Touchpoints

Andrew Rees

The Reading Glass Books
(888) 420-3050
production@readingglassbooks.com

Table of Contents

Foreword

A short story book moves quickly from one setting and group to the next, but allows the writer to present a wealth of ideas and the reader in turn to appreciate them. I called this book 'Touchpoints' because the themes of each story radiate out like light beams, able to connect with the reader's experience and insight. I hope that something in one or more of them has impact for you, be it Stephanie's exploration of the ocean depths, Simon's strength in handling the devastation of separation, Sonia's agonising over making a decision, or James' inability to switch off on holiday. And how about the weather, a subject we all know something about?

The book explores our feelings in a range of situations. It looks at different aspects of pain – grief for a friend or lover, sudden separation, the corrosive effects of captivity, and the devastation of setbacks. You may inwardly smile over the recollection of childhood memories, or the online society that follows us everywhere. Twelve stories, each painting its cameo and interconnecting with others, provide the background.

Thanks to Lottie for her careful proof reading.

No character in these stories is intentionally modelled on a known person.

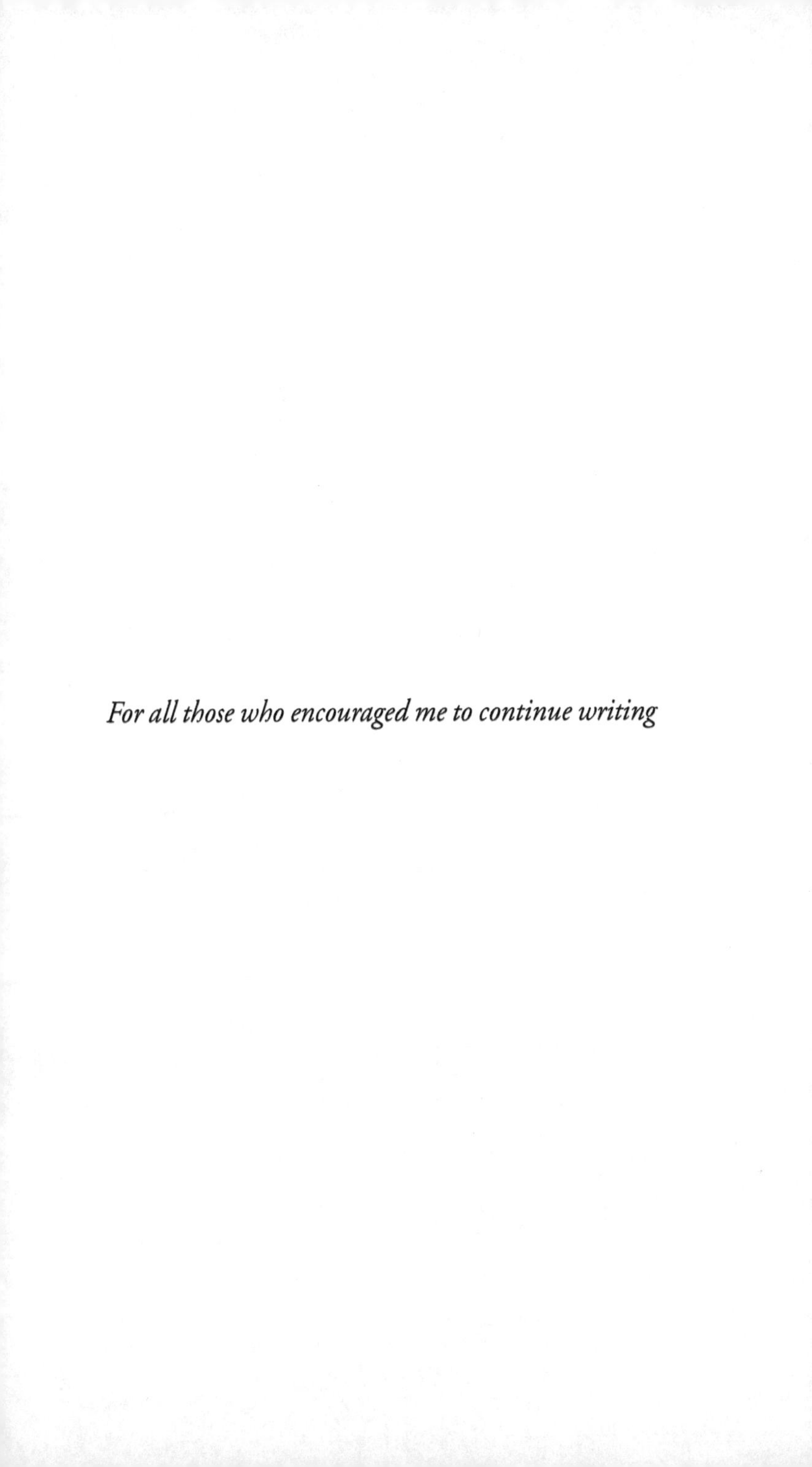

For all those who encouraged me to continue writing

The Book Cover

The church smelt damp, its dark, cold, rather unwelcoming interior serving as a backdrop to the event it was about to host. Why was it that funerals had to be solemn, dismal occasions, with everyone dressed in black, looking uncomfortable and sitting in silence? Brief nods of acknowledgment across the pews to family members not seen in years, and not likely to be seen till the next funeral. Aunt Audrey and Uncle Phil affecting a closeness to the deceased that they had neither experienced nor sought over the decades. And then there were the sides of the family that didn't get on, sat far apart and didn't speak to each other. Old enmities not softened in any way by the passing of the beloved parent or relative that they had in common.

For John, now, shocked at this sudden passing, it could be like walking into a minefield to say goodbye to his old chum, Patrick Brooks. Did he sit left side or right, near to people he didn't know, or find some reassurance in sitting alone, as if shielded from factional interest? He was saved by spotting Mrs Chandler, Patrick's neighbour, the one person he did know, who smiled briefly as he approached her and sat down. Looking ahead, he could see the flower-laden coffin in front of the pulpit, bringing home the finality of death. Inside it was Patrick, never to say another word, or walk another step. And soon even it would cease to exist, as it slid through a crematorium furnace. Dust to dust indeed.

John looked round briefly. There were just over twenty people seated, most strangers to him. All stood as the sound from the organ swelled, and the vicar in his robes walked in. 'Dearly beloved, we are gathered here today to say farewell'. He must have said this hundreds of times.

Funerals ran to an expected format with little variation, hardly honouring the richness and diversity of each human life. Three hymns, some words and prayers from the vicar and a brief eulogy from a family friend that barely did justice to Patrick's achievements, most of which lay unvalued and forgotten.

John felt he could have done better himself – at least mentioned Patrick's work on the St Albert fault line, at its time a breakthrough in geological research with the discovery of a third fault line in the Western Pyrenees. No, all they got was 'he studied Geology for many years and was on the staff at Birmingham University.'

Remembrance without reflection on the kind of life he had lived, with no sense of the energy and vitality that burst through into his work, no touchpoints to raise a wry smile as people recognised the man from the speech. Indeed from the general mood, no smiles at all. The man who had filled lecture halls to capacity in his US tours, now farewelled by a small group of people, mostly there for politeness. A poignant moment indeed, but passing by unappreciated.

Soon, after struggling through the final hymn, the bleak occasion was all over. Since only family were invited to the crematorium, John walked Mrs Chandler back to the large Victorian house where she lived on the ground floor, the top flat of which had belonged to Patrick. He wrapped a thick scarf around his neck to keep out the December cold. They walked past the town's street decorations. It was five days before Christmas.

'I'm not sure who will come to clear his flat. That was his daughter there, on the right, but she's come down from Scotland. I don't think there was any other child. Those others were university people,' she remarked.

'I wonder what they'll do with his collections? They should go somewhere but he fell out with Birmingham,' commented John. Patrick's boxed rock samples filled an entire room in his flat.

As recently as last week he had walked this street to have his regular Tuesday coffee and chat with Patrick, his friend of many years. All had seemed well, in fact he was unusually chatty, though as ever reflecting on the past rather than hoping for the future. John had even stayed an extra half hour. Then two days later Mrs Chandler had called him with the shock news – a massive stroke. She used to check on Patrick, and was alarmed when she didn't get a response. When the police broke into his flat, they found him already dead. Yes, he was seventy seven years old, but it was still a blow.

It seemed too hard to just walk back home, so at her invitation, John stayed for a cup of tea with Mrs Chandler, admiring how tidy her flat was compared to Patrick's upstairs. Her immaculately fitted red carpet contrasted with Patrick's threadbare rugs in the same room three floors above.

Conversation was hesitant, as if half the communication was silent, one thinking about a dear friend, and the other a pleasant neighbour.

'I'll miss him, he was an old style gent, always polite and helpful,' she started.

'Oh yes,' said John.

'Can never understand why no one ever visited him. He never spoke much about his daughter. They came to the funeral all right. Wouldn't have hurt them to have spent more time with him.'

John had a feeling this had been another falling out, but said nothing. Patrick had never spoken well or shown any pride in her.

'What's family if they can't be with you?' Mrs Chandler emphasized the point.

'Indeed.'

'You'll miss your Tuesday visits I expect?'

'You're right, I will. It'll leave a gap.'

'Cold in that church,' said Mrs Chandler. 'Glad to get home.'

'Yes, bitter.'

John found himself just making polite conversation, but in reality there was no conversation to have. The finality of the death of someone you saw regularly left an unfilled void, maybe not unfillable as time passed, but for now it left a feeling of verbal and mental numbness.

While reluctant to leave the warmth of her lounge, he felt he should get going.

'Thanks for the tea. I'll call by sometime,' he said, knowing full well that this was highly unlikely.

She saw him out, and he took a longer route home, hardly focussing on anything. He was dimly aware of some carol singing by the big Christmas tree in the shopping mall. 'Silent Night' wafting over the air, no doubt to encourage a festive mood and bring in more shoppers. He didn't intend to be tempted himself. Christmas, in his opinion, saw a shocking waste of money by encouraging gift buying for the sake of spending, rather than to consider possible usefulness for the recipient. How much of what was received was really wanted and used, rather than stored in a cupboard to pass on to the next person? Yes, we all want to be generous, but better a gift of low value or a gift token than the extravagance so often shown.

Yet being unwilling to go home immediately, he paused to look in the windows and something caught his eye. A picnic basket with neatly stacked white plastic plates, cups, and cutlery. He assumed this would be an outrageous price but saw it discounted at £12.99 and decided to buy this for his seven year old granddaughter, Sophie. The cashier wrapped it carefully in silver paper, and put it in a carrier bag. He walked away, looking at other windows but not being tempted to purchase anything more. One thing about Christmas was that it took your mind off life's worries. Gifts, carols, decorations, mince pies and mulled wine hardly threatened anyone. The comfort of the festive warmth was always welcome.

When he was young, John had loved Christmas – the surprise of gifts, guessing what might be inside the wrapping paper of the packages under the tree, the turkey lunch, pulling crackers and seeing his father wear a silly hat. All were memories that brought an inward smile. Buying presents for the family with his pocket money, trying to be meticulously fair with the money spent on each one. And then the Boxing Day trip to the cousins, comparing gifts, more food, black and white films on TV, and party games. They were older and had gifts that John could only imagine getting. After that it was seeing friends, and continuing the buzz until New Year. The worst part was the anti-climax of the decorations coming down on January 2nd, and then returning to school. You could almost cry that it was all over.

Now in his seventies, John was more circumspect. Some modest decorations brightened his home, but no tree, and only a few gifts, bought mainly for his three grandchildren. His annual walk to midnight mass had given way to watching it on TV instead. Then it was Christmas Day at his daughter's house close by, and Boxing Day in his own home with his son's family. They lived further away and hence came to visit him. Once that was done, life went back to normal, and he wasn't particularly sorry. Even his food was more modest – no Christmas pudding, chocolates, only a small cake, and chicken replacing turkey. None of the over indulgence of his younger years. He still couldn't quite understand why people ate and drank so much. One bottle of wine with Christmas Day lunch did it for him.

And so he made the rest of the journey home, his thoughts having moved on somewhat from the funeral. Yet while Christmas softened the impact of returning home, the blow of his friend so recently gone was still keenly felt. Usually once and sometimes twice a week, he'd called on Patrick, and while John was well connected locally, with a wide circle of friends, it would still leave a hole in his social life. It still didn't feel quite real, as if Patrick might return any minute. The impact wouldn't be felt till a few weeks later.

To keep busy, he rang his daughter and arranged for her to bring the children over late afternoon. Then he picked up the paper, and started reading it, but nothing grabbed him and he felt unable to focus on anything. Reflection on death by definition meant also reflection on life, and seeing it a bit differently than before. It was as if some of life's routine habits and happenings didn't really matter anymore, but we were still too lost to know what did matter. A kind of vacancy took over, as he sat in the armchair staring into space, his mind too powerful to let him move. Death also served as a reminder of his own mortality. At seventy two he wasn't getting younger, and a sudden stroke or heart attack could happen to him at any time, although his health was generally good. He was a keen walker and still cycled. But you just never knew.

Eventually he fell asleep for a few hours, and woke just before 4pm, feeling embarrassed about the time he had wasted. He did some tidying up, and soon his daughter arrived with the grandchildren. He talked to the two of them, Sam aged five and Sophie aged seven, about what Santa would bring them, listening to their excited answers, and trying to keep up with the long list they recited.

'Are you certain Santa can remember all of that? He's an old man and you may need to explain some of these things to him,' he asked them.

'Santa knows everything Grandpa. Besides he's got elves to help him,' said Sam confidently.

'Ok I see, but remember he's very busy. He has to get to all the boys and girls in one night.'

'Santa's smart. He can do all that super quick.'

There was no deflecting their confidence in the process. He was hoping that he might be doing his daughter a few favours by making them think a bit harder about what they wanted, but it was no use. They had an answer to everything.

It was the tonic John needed, however. He was amused by the conversation. Something about how the very young and old don't need to worry about bigger problems, leave that to those in mid-life. Christmas certainly put pressure on parents, with the dreaded December last delivery deadlines set by the retail websites. He glanced at Julia his daughter. She smiled knowingly, suggesting everything was in control.

'Tea, Dad?'

'Yes please, make a pot,' he said gratefully, comforted by the thought of them staying a while.

He started to tell her about the funeral, how it left him empty and didn't do credit to the real person. A funeral was for the living. The final act of appreciation before the deceased was committed to memory. A bringing together of a group of people who had one thing in common – the deceased person. Yet sometimes the living didn't do him or her justice. There was something unfinished, uncommunicated which needed to be understood or else it was forgotten forever. Like looking at the book cover without reading the book.

Julia nodded, and tried to help.

'Well I guess we all have to go sometime. At least he lived to his late seventies.'

'He was his own worst enemy at times, but he deserved more,' reflected John.

Talk quickly moved on to the practicalities.

'Who will clear out his flat if he knew so few people?'

'I really don't know. Family I suppose,' he said.

They stayed an hour and left. It had been nice to share, but now it was early evening and thoughts soon returned to his friend. He started up the laptop and googled: 'Patrick Brooks'. There were a few different individuals so named, but the fourth one down stood out:

'Patrick Brooks, Professor Geology Dept, Birmingham University, 1977-92. Well known for his work on the rock structures of the Western Pyrenees, proposing the theory that these Paleogene formations, resulting from the collision of the Iberian and European plates, had been subject to earlier shearing than was previously thought, including a lower fault line visible from caves in the area south of Lourdes. His book: 'Pyrenean Stress Fractures - St. Albert Fault Line' is now the acknowledged text book in the field. Professor Brooks has completed several lecture tours in USA, the last of which was in 1996.'

Yes this was more like it – the doorway into a past life. You began to see his depth, his passion, glimpses of the energy he threw into his work. The regular visits to Darosta each Easter and summer for years with the team of four or five from Birmingham that went with him, some for several years continuously. The contacts Patrick had made and remade at Bilbao to share his findings. The early starts to the day followed by evenings spent documenting the day's findings, and storing the samples in strict location sequence.

Like a tidal surge the fascinating tales Patrick had told him, now recollected, gathered force and were about to burst over John now. How the folds in Saint Pastiere formations had been matched to similar ones twenty miles further west, the belief that there must have been a major fault line, and then after two years searching, confirmation of a deep shear line in the nearby caves. The joy of discovery. It had been written and re-written on Patrick's face as he had retold the story. They had been real enough memories to those other field workers in the past too, but each had moved away and moved on. They probably didn't even know he was dead. John doubted that a Death Notice had been published in the national press, though word of mouth tended to travel fast once the universities heard.

Then there were the rock samples returned from numerous visits to Spain, each meticulously labelled, with photos and geographic co-ordinates, like an archaeologist archiving Egyptian relics. Frequently these had been brought out to show John, each small padded box containing a specimen that meant something to the trained eye, and each carefully annotated with suggested age, date of finding, location and photo of its background. Hours of painstaking work, that rightfully should pass to a geological society or university department. A man's lifework awaiting its fate.

Yet he was more than just a passionate academic. Patrick had been a family man and spent hours biking with his son, David. Overnight summer trips in the Pennines, carrying camping gear strapped to the back of the bike, taking the bare necessities to avoid excessive weight. Memories too of birthday parties in the family home, full and happy lives.

But then there had been the arguments, first with Birmingham who had refused to renew his post and offered the Departmental Professorship to an outsider. A real slap in the face. All this after a row over funding. Patrick may have been the white knight for the Department, pushing their interests, but the University took it badly. His manner was too blunt, parochial and self righteous for their liking. But worse was to follow, when David died in a car accident in 1997, a devastating blow that sapped his interest for everything. Then two years later, his wife left him, citing a dead marriage. It would have broken most men, but Patrick was ever dignified, taking early retirement and finding for himself a new life in a new place. It's not easy making new friends in your mid-sixties, and he wasn't outgoing by nature. John had met him through the Ramblers, admiring his extensive knowledge on country walks, and soon developed a friendship, but he was one of the few who got close.

Patrick was good at hosting, and his invitations to dinner or a drink at home were rarely expected to be reciprocated, and often refused by him if offered. You never saw him eating out or in the pub. Home soil was strength, and gave him space to open up and divulge details of his former life. John never found this boring, listening instead with fascination to detail of the '86 trip to Darosta, one of the more eventful. He warmed to this lonely soul. Bit by bit over the years, he built up the impression of this intense, thorough, kindly man, ready to open up if the situation was right. John had rarely needed to say much about himself, for there had been enjoyment in listening. They had settled into the Tuesday afternoon visit slot at Patrick's flat some years ago, supplementing it with other visits when appropriate.

John sat back in his armchair and let it all wash over him, as the silent book ran its course, maybe for the last time, and with the last person – a final act of appreciation, a journey of the mind. When he resurfaced, he realised it was late for dinner. Slowly, he put some soup in the saucepan and drank it with a slice of bread, to the accompaniment of the TV. This was beginning to feel better, the warmth of the soup matching a growing re-engagement with normal life.

Before bed, he realised he hadn't opened the mail. One item drew his attention and he opened a Christmas card showing a nativity scene, the infant Jesus with a halo round his head, watched by his mother and the shepherds. Yes what they say is true: one door closes and another opens. This was after all a festival about birth. Coming from the street, he could hear the strains of 'Silent Night'.

Searching

Coming here, alone, on a late afternoon in September, was the compromise Ed allowed himself. It had been a struggle at first, because this place so reminded him of his beloved Helen. She had worked for four months in "Felicity's", the restaurant on the left as you walked into the Pantiles from the south end. Now as on so many previous occasions, it was buzzing with families out on a Bank Holiday, with waitresses carrying trays full of pots of tea, cream cakes and ice creams. No tables free, and a small queue forming at the entrance. Some things never changed. No wonder she had got tired of being run off her feet and left.

Somehow he believed that walking where she had walked, where indeed they had walked together a few times after her shift, would act as some kind of therapy. It was all he could do. The concert halls they had visited, and places they had holidayed in over the eighteen months of their relationship, remained firmly out of mental bounds. Too sensitive and painful to visit on his own when he had known happier times with her. Playing cello in a professional orchestra had taken them all over the place, for the concert tour was demanding. Perhaps too many rehearsals and performances when they could have spent more time on their own. But there again, she had said that she loved them, and if it had given her joy, at the expense of more time together, it had been worthwhile. Anyway it was in the past, just as his role in that London based symphony orchestra had also finished once she left. Enough was enough. He didn't have the emotional energy to continue with it, despite his evident skills and widespread protestations from his colleagues.

On these occasions, they had walked the length of the Pantiles to the site of the chalybeate spring that had started the influx of visitors to Tunbridge Wells in the seventeenth century. You could look down at a pool of water and read the short history whose words were lovingly painted onto a black painted board. How different it had been four months ago, the last time they had done this walk, hand in hand, heading for his car, and driving to his cottage in Hartfield on the edge of Ashdown Forest.

Today in total contrast, he felt empty, lonely, purposeless, and stared into space until his mind refocused on the present, permitting him to continue his walk. The price of getting involved had been the price of pain, a pain they both would never have thought possible. But you never knew what was around the corner in life. There was no certainty in anybody being alive this time next year, however much they might choose to expect that. Somehow in his brokenness, he had to grasp something, to somehow move on in his feelings, and walking the same street slowly, while letting his mind search for the smallest recollection, was somehow helpful. It was better than staring at the four walls of the living room at Hartfield. There had been plenty of that recently, plenty of immobility, of working through a process of grief, of trying to understand the un-understandable.

They had returned from a week's holiday in Venice on the Saturday, after wining, dining and visiting the sites. Helen had posed in St Mark's Square with a happy smile for photos that he had minutely looked over since her death. In them, she had looked genuinely relaxed, content not tense, but was she really happy or just putting on a smile for the occasion? In hindsight it was her last week alive, making it all the more poignant. Ed had a habit of beating himself up with his doubts, but the more together you were with your partner in every meaning of the word, the more certain you could be of their feelings, and it had all felt good at the time. The piece of beauty before the fall.

On the Sunday, they had lain in bed late, slowly feeling their way back to autumnal reality, chatting and laughing, before driving to a local pub for Sunday roast. Then a leisurely afternoon watching a DVD box set. After that, the week kicked in and got busy. She had been moody, while he had been immersed in financial issues, and not too focussed on anything else. They had argued a few times over trivia, which in hindsight he regretted. She had talked about having to go back to her flat in Lambeth on Thursday, and of then joining him for his Saturday evening concert performance in the Barbican. Their parting early on that Thursday was in fact the final time he had seen her, an event of a few minutes that he had now picked over dozens of times. He remembered a quick kiss on the lips as she came to farewell him, and then the sound of the front door shutting. If only he had been a bit more attentive.

The phone call from the police had come that evening at around 7pm. They had found his number on her phone. The conversation was brief. Helen had been cycling over to a friend's place, and got crushed on the inside of a removals van as they both made a left turn at a roundabout. Ed had warned her about the dangers of cycling in London. This wasn't Amsterdam with the protection of clear cycle lanes. The city just wasn't set up for it, despite recent improvements. But she had smiled, doubtless believing that it wouldn't happen to her. 'Don't worry love, I'm always careful.' In truth she was a keen cyclist, having made the trip to Hartfield a number of times by bike.

Ed was at the hospital in an hour, but it was too late. Death had been instantaneous. The van driver had fitted mirrors but claimed he hadn't seen her. Ed wasn't interested in getting angry with him. His flower was crushed, its petals strewn. That was all that mattered. Nothing would bring her back. Man may have achieved much over the centuries, but couldn't touch the irreversibility of death.

It had been left to her family to visit the mortuary and arrange the funeral. At the church, he had played a solo cello passage with difficulty having almost pulled out in his upset state. The delicate task of honouring Helen, of building a dam wall against the tidal wave of his emotions, had nearly been too much. The family, her brother and mother, had been appreciative. He had joined the select group at the crematorium, before returning directly to Hartfield, and breaking down as soon as he got home. This was the finality of death. One day she was chatting to him over a mug of coffee in the kitchen, the next gone, never to return.

His mind ran over the largo of a Bach violin concerto, the beauty of the soul written into the violin passage, the first violin telling its message to the world, pouring out its love, hope and pain, before the second violin came in, its solo theme supportive of, rather than discordant with, the first. Together they made a piece of such beauty. The music of relationships, each supporting and enhancing the other, intertwined with spirit as they wrapped themselves around each other. The melody of love, each refusing to dominate in tempo or volume, for to do so would have destroyed the tension and the very message they were so effectively saying, ephemeral yet breathtaking.

Listening to the passage, the cello accompaniment of which he knew so well, had left him in tears, anchored to the armchair, helping him to express his loss, or at least find the nearest thing that could touch it. He had played it over and over again as the days passed. Ed was incapable of dealing with the business of clearing her possessions left in the house, leaving everything as it had been the day she had left, down to the position of the half opened jar of face cream in the bathroom. His usually busy schedule was cut cold. No more rehearsals or concerts for now. He would take a six month break. With his experience they would always be knocking on his door.

Would she have wanted this? Probably not, but for him the world wasn't normal any more. Maybe it was inherent in life that true beauty and happiness were things we only ever saw fleetingly, while most of our time was spent in the toil and frustration of everyday living. For now, he had to turn his back on the world, and handle this himself, staying close to anything that reminded him of her. If moving forward took months rather than weeks, then so be it. In time there would be the inquest, which he didn't have to attend, but would help him find closure. With it would come the anger directed everywhere – against the van driver, against those who didn't prioritise safer cycling, against life, against God. For now, there was the immediacy of the loss, which had led him today to drive into Tunbridge Wells, and, after walking and sitting for an hour, to return home.

'Ed Barnes meet Helen Turner.'

'Pleased to meet you Helen.'

'Likewise.'

It was another of Peter Shaw's weekend dinner parties, judiciously arranged on a Saturday night when there was a gap in the performance schedule, as he too played for the same orchestra, in the second violins. There were usually ten to a dozen people invited, his wife having prepared a wonderful array of dishes, while Peter focussed on opening three bottles of Beaujolais from his cellar. The guests varied on each occasion, being normally friends or family of fellow musicians.

'So what do you play Ed?' she had asked him, hoping the question was sufficiently broad to merit a full reply.

'Cello, played it from age ten. School orchestra led to studying music, then playing in local orchestras, bigger orchestras and here we are.'

'Your key to the big wide world.'

'Yes, I suppose you can say that. It's not a very small key I'm afraid. The bane of this instrument is its size, carrying it around, insuring it and so on. Flying can be a nightmare.' Ed smiled as he spoke.

'And has it brought you the life you wanted?' Helen continued to probe.

'How long have you got?'

'As long as you like…'

The chemistry was already working. Easter had been the following week and allowed him time to visit her flat. They had spent the whole weekend together. To Ed, after the breakup with his wife two years previously, and long periods of activity when he really had no time to look for anyone else, it felt perfect. The depth and quality of communication was phenomenal, almost as if she could read his mind. They moved effortlessly into meeting two to three times a week, before eventually she came down to Hartfield to live with him.

'Come in Mr Barnes… yes, I heard about your friend's accident, and offer you my deepest sympathies.'

It was two weeks after the visit to the Pantiles, and Ed was calling on Rev. Ian Francis at the vicarage of All Saints Parish Church in Hartfield, hoping that another view of grief might help.

'Thanks for your time vicar.'

'Do you feel able to tell me something of how you're feeling?'

Ed came straight to the point. 'It's been agony. She was here one day and gone the next. We had got on so well together. She had that calming, healing effect on me. We always had happy times whatever we did and wherever we went.'

'Yes, yes of course…' The vicar's soft tones, intended to draw out reluctant responses from visitors, took a back seat while Ed continued.

'It's the suddenness of it… just leaves you numb. All the things I enjoy, like my cello playing, were so bound up with her. She would come to all my concerts. I feel all purpose has been taken out of my life. I can't focus on anything. I feel so lost.' Ed's eyes filled with tears as he verbalised his pain.

'That's all fully understandable. Tell me more about her.' The vicar was sensing that talking itself was a therapy.

'Helen was a light, happy soul, never down for long. She had an open friendly personality, slightly mischievous at times. Her family come from Enfield. She worked part time as an art teacher at a local college in Lambeth - evening classes, some private tutoring. She had a small flat there, and her own car, but used to go everywhere by bike. Just couldn't see the danger in weaving in and out of traffic. I used to worry about her, but she would just dismiss it.' Words came easily to Ed. He was opening up now.

'What's your daily pattern at present and how has this changed? Has anyone helped or seen you in the last five weeks?'

The vicar continued to let Ed do the talking. In his view, one of the main issues was that Ed had had to face grief on his own. Here was a mountain of information seeing daylight for the first time. Bringing it up to the surface was relieving the load on the teller. He already looked a bit brighter. When the flow finally finished, the vicar took his cue.

'Two things to say. First, it would help if you can find someone to share your thoughts and feelings with. Not necessarily every day, but you need a listening ear. You must feel better now than when you arrived just because you've told me all this. You've unburdened yourself. That's part of a very important process of owning your feelings by sharing them. Secondly, don't beat yourself up any more about lack of sensitivity in the last few days you had together. It sounds to me that you both had great times together, happier than many people I meet. She will have understood everything. You can rest assured of that. It takes energy away from what she would want you to do, and that's to move forward in your life, return to your career, and make it more challenging for her sake.'

He paused for a moment.

'However, vicars are not just social workers. I'm not going to be prescriptive right now, because I don't think you would respond to that, but I think it would help if we had a short prayer. You may have felt angry towards God, which most people do in your case, but He is there to help you in your onward journey if you will let Him.'

Ed consented, and so, Rev Francis held his hand and prayed with him.

Ed rose to leave.

'Thanks vicar.'

'Not at all – remember grief is like a rock. You can't shift the event of loss, just as you can't move a rock, but can adjust your attitude to it over time. That carries pain, and all we can do is support you in that process. It's also a very personal experience and affects different people different ways. Don't let anyone talk to you about the textbook. Anyway, come again if it helps. Oh by the way, here are some local phone numbers you may find handy for counselling and support.'

Ed walked away. It had helped. He wasn't sure how, maybe it was just the recognition. One step forward on the path of release.

Spring 2012: a warm May and a ten day holiday in Holland that had ticked every box. Helen had always loved the culture and colours of Holland – every imaginable colour of flower, and whole fields of reds, pinks, purples and yellows in the spring bulb fields.

They had spent five days in Amsterdam, soaking in its unique character of canals, gabled house fronts, little bridges, tourist cruise boats and bicycles. Helen had been keen for them to visit the Rembrandt and Van Gogh museums, while Ed's choice was to listen to a chamber orchestra in the famous Concertgebouw, where the names of famous composers ran round the ceiling edge of its historic auditorium. Evenings to remember with nice restaurants and small back street pubs serving lentebok beer.

'I should have brought my oil paints and canvas, love. There's so much to paint – blue of the sky and the red brick and white tops of the buildings reflected in the water. You can see a few people doing just that.' For Helen, art was about grabbing the moment. A mood captured in a photo or painting that you might never encounter again.

'Amsterdam has such character. I remember coming here as a student and seeing the sites. So many visitors around and such a friendly feel. Just one of Europe's great tourist destinations.' Ed reflected.

'So many museums too. The Dutch are so proud of their culture.'

Eventually they moved on, stopping in Haarlem to see the old church, its cobbled square, and explore its winding streets. Here they hired bikes, and headed for the coast, some five kilometres away. On the way back from the long straight sandy beaches, they found a large country estate at Elswout, and walked round the vast beech woodlands, where banks of moss descended to the stagnant waters of an old canal. The small white painted bridges across winding channels in the grassy fields attracted Helen, who again wished she had her pallet handy.

'It's so wonderful here. Look at that curving avenue of young beech trees. Someone had gone to a lot of trouble planting these two hundred years ago.'

'Yes, you've got the greens of the beech leaves with the dark reds from the copper beeches.' Ed observed. 'Then the purple of the rhododendron bushes, with the whites of the tall daisies and the yellow flowers up by the house.'

'You're getting a painter's brain my love.' Helen smiled, put her arms around Ed and kissed him on the cheek.

They stopped for tea in the Orangery enjoying the formality of its square tables and white tablecloths, before departing south to see the bulb fields at Lisse and eventually spending their final two days in The Hague.

Each day had brought a new taste, something new to enjoy together in unending sunshine. Everything had fallen into place so easily. Truly a holiday to remember.

Ed was getting out every day now, and gradually after eight weeks resuming his contact with humanity. It would be the New Year before he would return to the cello, and with a different orchestra, but the key word for now was 'movement'. Staying still, immobilised, and transfixed would allow wounds to grow. He had taken the vicar's advice to visit a trained counsellor twice a week, and was finding it helpful. Last week he had met Helen's family to put flowers in the small vase by the wall in which her ashes had been placed. They had spent time together afterwards, time to share and support. Her mother, who Ed had hardly known, was very helpful and accepted his invitation to visit Hartfield before Christmas.

At first, he had been dubious of the phrase 'do what Helen would have wanted'. It seemed to him an excuse for doing what you like, and then claiming justification from the unknown wishes of the dead. Often friends can be more certain than the deceased of what the latter really thought, which was probably as confused and uncertain as in anyone's mind. But then to act upon the phrase, to pause before action, was to defer to the departed, to consider their views, and remember them whatever the ultimate decision. That could only be healthy, as they live on in the hearts of their loved ones.

And so, Ed could begin to accept that it was better he move on, in work, in the community and to re-engage with friends. However, it might be a number of years before he could ever feel emotionally free enough to seek another relationship, if indeed he ever would.

He could rest content that Helen and he had enjoyed eighteen months with each other, and that at least was a cause for thanks rather than sorrow. He was now seeing his cup as half full, not half empty.

Departure

The torn off sheet of lined paper lay waiting on the coffee table. The writing was neat and clear to be sure that the message was fully understood, a last pause before a momentous exit. It could so easily have been sent as an email or text, but what was important here was timing – its message was not intended to be read until a number of hours later. Indeed, the later the better. A 'fait accompli' that became stronger with every passing minute. Conversely, it could have not been written at all. A phone call from a friend or relative would have been enough. Yet somehow, the need to write something, to engage in the finality of departure and to bring on an ending, became overwhelming.

Simon was surprised to find no one home when he turned the key in the front door. His three day business trip to Milan brought him home on a

Thursday night, expecting to see Marie, his partner of five years, there as she had implied in a morning phone call. The place was in darkness, so he thought at first she had gone out somewhere, and proceeded to carry his case into the bedroom. There he had seen the wardrobe door wide open, revealing its empty contents, and bare half closed drawers that had once been so full they were impossible to open. The dressing table had been cleared, bathroom cupboard likewise. The sickness of realisation dawned from the first moment he saw this. It had been planned and executed in every detail - nothing hurried, everything careful and deliberate. She must have filled several cases, some no doubt consigned to storage. Just the essentials taken with her.

It was only later, after checking the kitchen and spare room, that his eyes fell upon the note. Something told him not to read it. Whatever it said was bound to be painful, rubbing salt in the wound. But read it he must. It was carefully written in block capitals and in her hand:

'I'M NOT RETURNING, SO DON'T TRY AND FOLLOW ME OR CALL ME. I WILL BE SAFE. BRIAN WILL CONTACT YOU SOON TO SORT THE NECESSARY.'

There was nothing new here. Brian was her brother, and the implication was that she had gone back to Scotland to be with her family, since he had always lived near the family home just outside Dumfries. By now she would be half way there on an overnight train from Euston. He had already noticed that the car was parked in its usual spot in the front courtyard. It wasn't so much consideration that prompted that, as the sure belief that Marie didn't relish a four hundred mile drive. She had never been keen on driving. He had always done most of it.

He considered calling her anyway, but then thought it pointless. The number, once so easily and frequently rung, would now go straight to voicemail or be barred already. She would be sure not to answer. Besides, why play her game? She would know from the caller ID that he was now home and had discovered her departure. Why give her the satisfaction of knowing when that had happened?

He sat down on the settee, stopping to think. It was true that their relationship had eroded over the years they had been together; each, for a while now, leading self contained lives while living under the same roof. Marie was frequently away at friends, as if uncomfortable in his company, returning Sunday evening for the week ahead. Yet they still shared a bedroom, and a few evenings at home each week. This was a shock and there was no other way to take it. Nothing had been building towards this - no violence, no fury and bitterness, no worries over money. Life had been anything other than dramatic.

They had always talked through their problems big and small. Deterioration did not equal severance and in his eyes and there had been no clues to suggest that she thought otherwise. Maybe he was just naive, too buried in work to notice. Anyway, the finality was sinking in, a moment for him alone, not to be shared. There was no anaesthetic for this. The pain would play itself out slowly and inexorably over the coming weeks. Recovery, if one could think of such a word, was weeks if not months away, if indeed it ever happened.

Simon made himself do something. Thinking, when you were too numb to think, or didn't want to give yourself the opportunity to think, was something to avoid. He boiled the jug for coffee and found a ready meal in the fridge. Five minutes in the microwave cooked his lasagne. Sitting alone at the kitchen table, he ate slowly, the ten minute space it gave him being as important as the meal itself. The food tasted good, somewhat salty but the sauce gave it plenty of flavour. Being still hungry, he looked in the fridge for dessert, found a half finished flan, warmed it and continued eating. It put him in a somewhat better frame of mind. There was no point thinking anything, it was all too early. Who knows she might even return tomorrow?

But deep down he doubted it. This had been carefully planned and executed. The chilling feeling was how far back she had planned this. She must have sat opposite him for breakfast last week, thinking 'I've only got seven more days of this'. Maybe it went back months. He had a suspicion that she had involved someone else, probably a man to help carry her luggage downstairs, store the excess baggage and drive her to the station. He had a few ideas who, but didn't really care. Maybe it was one of her friends he had rarely met, or just a driver from a taxi truck company. He hoped the latter, as it would have been grossly disloyal for a mutual friend to get involved, and then have to avoid him ever after. That was too much to ask anyone. But then he was sure that someone they knew was 'in' on the plan. He didn't trust her to just to exit without saying goodbye to someone.

It was almost like being in a movie. The leading lady decides to leave, packs her bags, scrawls a note, and marches off into the night. Her husband arrives home in a happy mood only to find he is on his own now. We trace their separate onward journeys, one enjoying the freedom of change, successful in life, celebrated by friends, the other does it the lonely hard way, never fully recovering. The guess is that the wife is the former and the husband the latter, but it needn't necessarily be that way. He might find himself enjoying a freer life, albeit not by choice, while she finds the outside world a hard place. The intense craving to find drama in the lives of others, to watch their soap opera, makes this compelling viewing. Someone else to model our lives on. Sadly, life wasn't like that.

Strangely, he felt no anger towards her. That would come later. It was all shock for now, like a big cloud that enveloped his mind preventing him thinking clearly on anything else. Better to just do something else rather than think, but then you couldn't focus on anything. He stood for a moment asking himself if this was really happening. It was like wandering in a mist, surprised when objects or people appeared out of nowhere. Perhaps soon it would disperse and clear, allowing him to see more clearly and take a more rational view.

Eventually, Simon's first clear thought was to keep quiet about the split, until he was prepared to tell everyone. Why give others the satisfaction of knowing, of reaching for the phone to tell their friends, of having something to gossip about? Besides, by waiting for the reactions of friends, he could tell who she had already told. They had no immediate engagements with anyone, and some of them were away on summer holiday. Today was July 21st. He could keep clear of them all for the next six weeks without incurring suspicion. This was a private pain to bear. They had spoken of having a holiday, but Marie always got vague about the subject, and so nothing had been booked. He might take a week off soon, and just go away somewhere. Maybe to see Owen, his old school friend who now lived in the Preseli Mountains in Wales. Long walks across the hills and a few beers at night would be just the tonic.

The important point was not to feel defeated. Feel changed, yes. Change had been forced upon him, but that didn't have to be negative. Use the moment to take stock, to have some lazy days, to enjoy the sunshine, and do one thing each day that makes you feel happy. Tomorrow, Friday, wasn't a bad start. A short day in the office after the Milan trip and then two days of the weekend. Perhaps a drive to the coast, sit on the beach, take an excursion into the hills. It all sounded good, but was less inviting when you were doing it alone.

But then it had to be better than staying in the apartment where everything was a constant reminder of the absent Marie. And what would she be doing now? Most of the way to Scotland by now. No doubt, staying with her parents, extracting every ounce of sympathy and support, the smile of relief shining all over her face.

Simon turned on the TV for company. A documentary on nuclear power would have been interesting had he been more receptive. He flicked the channels. The first day of a Pro Golf tournament was on, and he watched it briefly, being one of the few things that penetrated his mind. He didn't play the game, but enjoyed watching the professionals line up and then execute their shots. It had a certain unhurried, laid back ambience, that seems unique in sport. No clock watching or arguments with referees, just the simple precision of hitting a ball into a hole. He watched twenty minutes and then switched it off. It was still a little early to retire for the night, but so he did. He needed to conclude this day, to forget it, and start another.

Friday was a short day in the office for Simon, followed by a return home to the scene of the departure. The note still lay on the table, a reminder that this wasn't a dream, wasn't going to go away. He picked it up and read it again, as if searching for tiny clues about her mindset. It was so carefully done, capital letters hiding the emotion. Cold, sharp, direct, concise, strong. Probably there were a host of other words to describe this message, written with reluctance as a necessary communication. It had no hint of concession or negotiation. Finality in a word. He was tempted to rip it up and throw it away, thus rejecting any hold she had on him. But then again, it might be useful to show the note to others later.

He wondered how and when the next conversation would be, and if he would ever talk to her again. They only had property to split, and she would surely avoid direct communication. Part of him wanted to leave everything as he had found it, to simply ignore it. She could write what she wanted, but he didn't have to agree or accept it. Maybe he should post it to her parents, to show them how she behaved. Perhaps it would embarrass her, she certainly wouldn't be pleased, though no doubt they had already fallen in with her tales of an unhappy life.

Then there was his own life to continue. He had no plans for the weekend, and it was only 3.30pm. He changed and thought about driving down to the coast, a journey of just over an hour. He needed the space, fresh air, the feel of a cool breeze in his face. A walk along the front at Eastbourne, past the parks, and beach amusements, followed by a fish supper seemed a good option. Nothing like a change, so he walked down the stairs to their (or was it now his) parked car, and drove away. The traffic was quite light as he took the windy lane over the hills, and before long he was there. It felt unusual to be driving alone, only the radio to keep him company. Being unsure where to park, he found a side street two blocks back from the beach, walked the short distance to the front, and onto the beach itself.

The crunch of his shoes on the shingle felt good, like taking the first hesitant footsteps in a new life. There were plenty of people around: families, couples. Each was a silent reminder to him that he was here solo, when everyone else wasn't. However, for now, it was more important to be outside, to go somewhere, and feel the optimism of the sun on your face. He sat down, letting the late afternoon sea breeze refresh him, as he watched children play round the groynes. The rhythm of the waves crashing on the beach, being sucked away and crashing again was somehow comforting. There were occasional variations as a stronger wave would reach further up the beach. Out at sea, two surfers were making a half hearted attempt to catch a wave.

It felt good to be here, exuding a sense of healing and stability. The sea had been here for thousands of years, and would still be here for thousands more, putting everything else into perspective. A realisation grew that he could sit here for hours if he wanted to. There was no one to meet, no reason to have to leave. Time passed, and the beach began to empty in the early evening. He would be here alone in an hour amid the gathering gloom of twilight and an incoming tide.

To his right was the familiar sight of the chalk cliffs at Beachy Head, looking more dramatic in silhouette against the fading light, and he reflected on previous walks up to East Dean, and round the cliff edge, overlooking the sharp drop down to the lighthouse below. It suddenly occurred to Simon that it was a good spot to jump off when life wasn't worth living. How many people must have looked down from the edge and thought 'shall I or shan't I?' in their desperation and agony. How many of those left notes behind, 'I couldn't take it anymore…', which were read when it was all too late. It put some perspective on Simon's case. There was always someone out there worse off than yourself.

The battle inside him wasn't there, at the cliff edge, yet. When it came to digesting the shock, he was still on the right side of the abyss. Was it that he was just different from Marie or just a person who was impossible to live with, with whom the next relationship would also degrade over time? Was it because of his lifestyle, maybe seen as too much into himself, or was it instead her unrealistic expectations of him? What could he learn or should he change? There was always something.

By degrees, daylight faded into twilight, and he began to look out of place, sitting aimlessly alone on a shingle bank when everyone else was going around with purpose. But he wasn't finished yet. As the numbness wore off, he needed to touch his emotions, to feel and face the pain. Marie wasn't coming back. The line had been crossed, and it was important to let go. There were still some feelings for her, nothing like he had had when they moved in together five years ago, but he had to accept this and go forward and not be paralysed in the moment. The abrupt manner of her departure hurt, but he wasn't devastated.

While it was tempting to be defensive, to try and protect himself from the pain of this unexpected slap in the face, he could honestly say he wasn't mortally wounded. Departure was a form of death, and what we often mourn is the loss to us. Noting that was important, to allow time to reflect on a part of his life now closed, but once done he had to move on. Maybe being here on the beach now was a form of silent observation, a time to let the feelings and memories roll out of him, as indeed they would continue to do so in the next few days.

Eventually he rose to his feet. He walked past a few fish restaurants before selecting one and sitting near the window for dinner. It was awkward being alone, seeing groups chatting away out of the corner of his eye. He fiddled with his phone, re-reading some emails that he had read in a hurry earlier, then checking the news. His haddock soon arrived and he was surprised how hungry he was. Old fashioned fish and chips with mushy peas, bread and butter and a pot of tea. When was the last time he had eaten that? Food that brought back memories of childhood, being out with his parents. It made him feel warm and comfortable, basking in the memories.

His first recollected seaside visit was a family holiday to Bournemouth. He must have been five years old and his sister three. He could remember making a big sandcastle with a trench around it filled with water. They had stayed at a beachfront hotel in a spacious room, playing card games each evening. Happy days. Quickly, he came back to the present, paid and left. It was not yet mid evening, so he took a walk up the front and on to the pier, looking back at the neon lights. He wasn't one for the game arcade but on this occasion indulged in the 2p slot machines, watching the coins tumble into the tray. Simple entertainment that took his mind off other things.

He walked on past the small shops and restaurants, and looked up to the night sky. It was a clear night, the stars shining brightly. Years ago he could have picked out Orion and the Great Bear, but now the patterns looked unfamiliar. It was strange how seldom we looked at the stars. Like everything else in nature, they were always there, but people rarely stop to observe how awesome the night sky really is. Slowly he made his way back to the car, and the drive home.

'Thank you for coming in Mr. Marshall.'

It was two weeks later, and he was sitting opposite Mrs Lamont, the regional organiser of the 'Blue Shield' charity shops. He had responded to an advert requesting weekend voluntary help.

'Can I ask how you found us?'

'I saw your advert in the Daily Courier and since I'm free most weekends, I thought I'd like to help.' Simon figured that doing something different would be a step in the right direction.

'Good, have you worked in a charity shop before?'

'No I haven't.'

'OK, let me explain. The nearest shop to you is at Tonbridge. Mrs Glover runs it and needs help with sorting the boxes people bring in. We separate books, toys, garments and so on. Some items are in bad condition and have to be disposed. There are categories of items we don't accept, for example perishable items. The shifts are 9 to 1 pm, and 1 to 5 pm Saturday. We need volunteers for both, so you can decide which you prefer. The work can be quite busy, particularly Saturday morning. If you can't make a Saturday, as everyone needs some weekends off occasionally, please give a week's notice so we can find cover. We sometimes get people needing help unloading boxes from their vehicle, so there's lifting involved. How does all that sound?'

'Fine, I can handle all that.' There was nothing here that challenged Simon.

'That's good. There are other roles in the shop– pricing, restocking and the cashier. Over time you would get to do these, but if you start with sorting, you'll get an idea how we work. We also need to do a police check on you which should take ten days. After that I'll ask Mrs Glover to give you a call. You may want to call her or meet her at the shop before you start.'

'OK, sounds good, I'll wait to hear.'

'Thank you so much. We depend on volunteers like you. I think you'll find it rewarding.' Mrs Lamont stood up, smiled, and shook his hand.

And so it was arranged. Something that Simon would never have thought of doing while living with Marie, was now about to become reality. It meant more as a change of direction in life, than the amount of time or effort he was committing. From banking to community service. He had no high expectations. This was filling time with doing a task he considered worthwhile, yet which also gave him back something he so badly needed: a pillar round which to structure his empty weekends, a chance to meet new people, and an involvement with his community. It seemed that more and more people used charity shops in these times of recession. For him, 'doing' time meant less 'thinking' time, and that was best for now. He was pleased. It seemed a positive step and who knew where it might lead?

In the two weeks since Marie left, he had heard nothing from either her or her brother. In due course there was the issue of either buying out her share of the apartment, or selling it. He had thought vaguely about the former, but was beginning to think that selling and making a new start might be better for him, a way to wipe away the memories and move forward. Being on his own now gave Simon a freedom he didn't have before. It might have taken a blow to get it, might have been something he wasn't seeking, but it was now his opportunity. Yet freedom was no good unless you did something with it, changed your life and changed yourself. That was the key, to keep moving, be open and not to recriminate. It needed strength, and could be painful, but it was the only way. Recovery was still well into the future. Some people never recovered when their partner walked away. It left a hole that never got filled, a pain for which there was no relief.

For the first time since it happened, he could afford a smile.

Trip Of A Lifetime

'How about Hong Kong?'

Been there twice, seen Victoria Harbour, climbed the Peak, taken a boat out to Lantau.'

'Oh… Ok. Let me see. Delhi?'

'Spent two weeks there with George… Red Fort, Jama Masjid Mosque, Lodi Gardens, India Gate.'

His knowledge was encyclopediac. Henry could probably tell you what he did on each Wednesday afternoon when he was in each place, and there was surely nothing he had missed in the many cities and countries he had visited. Every attraction attended, every experience sampled. There was, of course, no reason not to go again. The India of his twenties was a different place now, thirty eight years later. It would be interesting to see these places again, as he approached retirement, but he was a great one for ticking the box. Been there, done that, let's go on to something new.

For Pat, who was much less travelled than her husband, it was an exercise in pleasing Henry as much as herself. As they planned a retirement trip, her main interest was to make him happy. She had travelled round France and Switzerland some years ago, but in reality, spent all her holiday time in UK where they lived. Henry had been the instigator for this trip, constantly referring to a holiday away as the reward for his retirement. She preferred him to take the lead, as wherever they went, it would be outside her comfort zone. They were in the early stages of planning it all. In two months he would be retired, age sixty two, and they planned to be away eight weeks, destination uncertain. To narrow that uncertainty, Pat was thumbing through Travel Agent catalogues and checking out various websites.

'Don't forget your cousin in Wellington. You could see him.'

'Richard? I haven't seen him since I was ten. Haven't heard from him for at least five years.'

This was the other problem. Henry could be quite stubborn and unfriendly. What did it matter if you haven't seen a distant cousin in ages? It's hardly a snub if he lives on the other side of the world. All it took was a phone call. Richard would probably be overjoyed to see them.

'Velta Worldtours are doing a Pacific cruise, sounds ideal: Western Samoa, Fiji, Tahiti, Cook Islands, ending up in Hawaii.' Pat was hoping Henry would like it. The pace sounded ideal for her, the much clichéd 'trip of a lifetime.'

But he was not to be drawn. Henry had a loathing for packaged holidays, for which cruises were, in his eyes, another example. They symbolised captivity – set meal times, making polite conversation with other guests, short stopovers, organised entertainment. As a way to holiday, it was bottom of his list. Deep down, Pat knew that too, but since it hadn't been mentioned for a few years, she had wishfully hoped that his views might have changed. One look sideways at him reminded her without him having to say anything. Nothing was different.

'OK Henry, I give up. You suggest somewhere.'

'To be honest, I haven't given it a thought. Asia sounds good. I'll check out China.'

For Pat, this put the discussion back in the box. Henry might like the idea of going to China, but there would be little chance of him checking anything out unless she kept on at him, morning, noon and night. This was going to need planning from a distance away, so it wasn't too early to start. He was just one of those individuals riddled with contradictions, wanting to see places, but unwilling to do the detail, plan the itinerary and make all the preparations. Suddenly, late in the day, he would give it all total focus, and then everything would go into high stress while last minute arrangements were hurriedly put together.

'Well make sure you check it out soon. It's the last week of June now, and we want to be away by early September. Hotels do get booked up, you know.'

She was sure her comments would fall on deaf ears. Nothing would be said for three weeks, he would focus on leaving work and they would be restarting the discussion in a month's time.

'Don't worry so much about it, everything will be ok. We'll fly business class, stay in a five star hotel. It'll be the best holiday you've ever had.'

Henry's tone seemed patronising, but he didn't mean it to be. He had a big picture in mind – retirement in three weeks and then all the time in the world to do whatever he wanted. They could go away wherever and whenever they pleased, be that September as suggested, or next spring. With two adult daughters to look after the house and dog, they could be away two months or six. It had been over thirty years since his last long distance travels, so he would savour the opportunity and enjoy every minute.

Deep down he was a nineteenth century pith helmet explorer. Map, compass, water bottle and rucksack were the tools he had used in his twenties, when touring India with his friend, George. Taking local buses to remote locations, going out of his way to talk to people, ask information, buy local food from stalls, play the extrovert and make people laugh. One such journey he fondly remembered was the visit to the Makipura Temples. They had travelled six hours by bus to a remote village, where after some inquiries they had found a room for the night.

The following day they hired bicycles, and having checked directions, set off. The route took them along a river valley where they waded the river, holding the bikes up high, and then along tracks that eventually led to dense undergrowth and a long overgrown dilapidated wall. Where it had fallen down, they climbed into a courtyard which looked as if it hadn't been seen in decades. They could make out old temple buildings in various stages of decay, and pulled away a thicket to reveal the statue of a goddess - Kali, they supposed. It looked perfect in the afternoon sunlight, as if unwrapped for the first time.

Encouraged, they walked over to a low doorway and once inside they could see, by match light, paintings on the walls, and small stone statues on a shelf. This felt like discovering a pharaoh's tomb, an abandoned temple waiting to be viewed with new eyes. It had fallen out of use and been allowed to decay. Inspired, they took photos and wrote some notes, as if rediscovering it for the first time. Something for the photo album or scrapbook. It had been the highlight of the entire trip.

Henry had been in his element – confident, enthusiastic, intrepid, though they had rarely been in any danger. The holiday had continued for three months, working north through the sub continent. They had seen the beaches of Goa, the burning ghats of Varanasi, the Thar desert of Rajasthan. Each day had been fascinating, producing the unexpected, seeing new sights, and making easy friendships in the many places they visited. Eventually the money ran low, even though they lived cheaply. Coincidentally, it was time to start university, and so reluctantly they returned to London. But the wonderlust was planted forever. There had been a few other trips over the years, notably ten days in Hong Kong in his thirties, but nothing on the scale of the great Indian adventure.

Travelling with Pat would, of course, be different. He knew that. At sixty two years, he wasn't about to set off into the wilds, but the awe of Asia still gripped him. He had never been to China, other than Hong Kong, and so now the prospect of seeing the Great Wall, Forbidden City in Beijing, tombed warriors of Xian, and the modern city of Shanghai, appealed to him. The difference in culture, language, tradition between China and the West was huge, and if holidays were about experiencing something completely different, this was it for him.

There was also the option of heading south or west from Beijing into areas off the tourist beaten track, where you could experience the real 'vibe' of the place. This was vital for Henry. Meeting and mixing with the local people was the real experience. All you needed was a few words in their language. They would teach you the rest, just as they showed you the local dishes, letting you sample a few before opting for your chosen dinner. And all this set against the backdrop of laughter, role play, even singing.

Henry trusted that his old skills from India were still usable after all these years. People loved easy humour: it transmitted well, building friendships and confidence. In fact, the complete antithesis of sipping gins at the bar of a five star hotel and making forced conversations with other western couples. It wasn't that Henry in any way despised that, far from it, but it wasn't what he came for. The joy of talking with local people, making a fool of yourself to win their trust was, for him, being in the present. Save the five star hotel till the last few days before the flight home.

So for now, fear held him back. The fear that the holiday he dreamed of having wasn't the holiday he was going to get. He was sure Pat would enjoy it, as everything would be new to her - a trip to the markets, coffee in an outside cafe, and riding on the local bus or ferry would satisfy her. But he needed something more, to step away from the islands of comfort, and explore. Yes that was it, explore. Jump on a bus or train and take a ride out of town. See an off road village, walk along a remote beach, climb a hill to get a good view. These were the activities he needed, but given his age, the need to look after her, and the lack of a good mate to join him, they were also the activities least likely to happen.

Deep down, he knew that, but hated to admit it. He would find himself in the hotel bar beside Pat for want of anywhere else to go, but better this than nothing. Staying at home one month after retirement would be a dreadful anti-climax. It wasn't about being selfish either, he was happy to spend some of the time doing just what she wanted, but it was a recognition that they were different people with separate interests. Those differences always came to the surface when you travelled together, as if free time brought out the real person.

Contrary to her view, he did actually research the places and produce an itinerary. Time was a commodity they had in plenty. They could afford three to four days in each place they stopped in, including a week in Malaysia on the way out. Enough time to go down to Singapore, take a ride round the harbour in a junk, visit the Raffles Hotel to drink the famous Singapore

Sling, and walk around Chinatown. That still left time in Kuala Lumpur to see the Petronas Towers and other sights. Travelling was about forgetting the urgencies, not having to be somewhere at a certain time any more than you could help. It was about seeing something or somewhere you like and not having to say 'no I don't have time to spend another day there'. About going with your feelings.

A favourite saying of Henry's was 'take the chance now, you never know when it may recur.' The sense of being in the moment was everything. If you looked too far ahead or too far back, you missed the beauty of now. The remembrance of that moment would be less vivid in later years, a missing link to a happier life. Focus on the here and now, as if the past was nothing and the future undecided. That was the best option, there was no other way.

And so the schedule began to emerge, from the first day landing in Kuala Lumpur. He figured around six weeks would be enough. If they left in September, they would be back by early November and he knew that Pat's Christmas planning started early each year. It was discussed and agreed the following week. He left her to talk to the Travel Agent and make the bookings.

Piece by piece, the trip came together. Flights, hotels, local tours, which Henry for all his independence recognised were necessary. The schedule was to fly to Kuala Lumpur, take the train to Singapore, then fly to Beijing, Shanghai, Xian, Chengdu (to satisfy Henry's desire to get off the tourist trail) a brief stay in Hong Kong (to which, as Henry kept saying, he had already been), and finally fly to Seoul and Tokyo.

'How long do you want to stay in Beijing?' Pat asked him, in one conversation typical of many.

'I think allow a week. There's the Forbidden City and Beihai Park, that's one day. The Summer Palace is huge that's another, Temple of Heaven and the Hutongs a third, Great Wall and Ming Tombs a fourth, markets a fifth. May as well make it a week.'

'OK, love. Are you happy with the hotel, it's close to Tiananmen Square, very central.'

'Yes, it's fine.' Henry wasn't sure that it was fine, but wasn't prepared to spend time looking at alternatives. It would do.

There had been some hard compromises to make. Pat was uneasy about spending too much time in China, so Henry's cherished visit to Chengdu had been cut to four days. This allowed time for the group photo of them both with local villagers that he so wanted. His dreams had a habit of being outdated and unrealistic, and she suspected this would be no exception, but was content to let the situation run its course.

The six weeks was enough time also to see something of South Korea and Japan. Henry had pored over the atlas, and decided a bullet train ride from Tokyo to Kyoto was the way to go. This was one of the oldest cities in Japan, full of old temples, so well worth a visit. From Tokyo, their final destination, they would return to London on an overnight flight, arriving at Heathrow on a cold grey November day. That would bring them down to earth, but the memories would linger. You couldn't take those away whatever happened later on.

Once booked, their mid-September departure was only four weeks away, and the practicalities of vaccinations, clothes shopping, compiling information, and making arrangements over the house, swung into place. Each day saw them draw a step nearer, with Pat taking the lead. Henry, true to character, was quite blasé about the preparations. He would only move into high gear once they were two to three days away from September 17th, their departure date.

The ambulance came at 4 am.

Henry had been quite vague during the previous two days, and on getting up in the night to walk to the bathroom had collapsed, his left leg and arm drained of strength. It was evidently a stroke that had been building for some time. Maybe the pressure of the impending trip had brought it on. Whatever the reason, he was now being rushed to the King Alfred Hospital with Pat by his side. It was September 13th, four days before they were due to leave. Now they would be going nowhere.

Once admitted into intensive care, Henry was given the required clot busting drugs, and left to stabilise. He was checked hourly. By morning he had regained some speech, but his left arm was still unresponsive. It would be a long haul to recovery.

Pat had been too busy with the visits to think about the holiday for two days. She had exceeded the visiting hours, though the hospital didn't seem to mind. The house seemed a lonely place on her return until Jo, one of their daughters, had come over.

Eventually, she contacted the agent and the full round of cancellations was started. A reluctant admission of defeat for what had become a much anticipated event. At least the stroke had happened now, and not when they were away, grappling with language as well as hospital systems in a foreign country. But there was really no comfort in any of this. For Henry, once he returned home, there would be a long slow road of remedial treatment, and a list of drugs that would be with him the rest of his life. It was numbing and depressing.

Pat was beyond tears. The current emergency acted like a lid of a pressure cooker, preventing her true feelings from being expressed. If you had asked her in June what she felt about a six week holiday in Asia, she wouldn't have cared. But now they were days off departure and she had grown to like making arrangements to visit far off cities that had meant nothing to her before. She had read up on China, imagined the mysteries that lay behind the successive walled courtyards of the Forbidden City and the underground terracotta army buried by an Emperor in preparation for the afterlife. Each purchase of a new dress, bag or medical kit had inched her one step closer. It was like an escape, a once only experience into another world, an awe inspiring place of such difference, a pallet of new tastes and colours. The kitchen door had been opened, and the smell of cooked turkey wafted out. Now it was slammed shut and the turkey thrown away. To risk getting close now was to flirt with disappointment.

Not only was this taken from her, but she had a new and painful situation to handle. It was cruel that Henry, just retired, and in his early sixties, should be struck down like this. Coming to terms with his restricted situation would be tough for him. He wasn't used to taking life easy, resting at home with slow days. He had no established pattern of daily living in retirement yet, having only just left work. There was always the risk of stroke recurrence if he got stressed with his condition, which, knowing him to be stubborn by nature, was a highly likely outcome. It was really a no win situation that she now had to work on to make it tolerable for all.

It was a week before Henry could focus on anything other than his physical condition. Some feeling had slowly returned in his left arm, but his left leg was still weak and there was no way he could leave hospital until he could walk. He was desperate to gain strength and get home, but nothing could be hurried, and even his impatient nature began to understand that. The loss of the holiday didn't even register with him for a week. Yes, he had looked forward to renewing his acquaintance with Asia, but the Asia he loved was that of his twenties and thirties.

He already knew, despite his hopes, that somehow he would be curtailed, that his dream no longer existed and to chase it to China would yield little or nothing. Instead, he must expect to submit to someone else's schedule – where to catch the plane, train, bus, when to eat dinner at the hotel, what time to be ready for the next day's action. It wasn't a world he could control, and sensing that became one way to handle the disappointment.

It was true he had wanted to go away, talked about it often over dinner during the last few years, but while it sounded good, it was never quite his dream. Who wouldn't want to go away as soon as they retired? It was the magnet that kept you going at work, month in, month out. Once you got closer, however, the gloss started to fade. He had gone along with the arrangements, helped with the schedule, but his doubts had begun to surface. The idea had served its purpose, and now rather than feeling the pain of having it snatched away, he really had no strong feelings about it.

It took three weeks to get Henry home, and a schedule of home visits kept him under constant attention. His one aim was to get back to where he had been with his health, unable to accept that things had changed forever. Retirement was no longer about an alternative active life after the stress of the workplace, but instead a change of pace and lifestyle, of slower deliberate speech, staying at home and only doing local walks. He was slow to accept that.

'Would have been nice just to see the Great Wall,' said Pat one day.

'You can see videos on line – same thing,' he replied.

'No it's not. Being there is best. Oh well one day, perhaps.'

Solitary

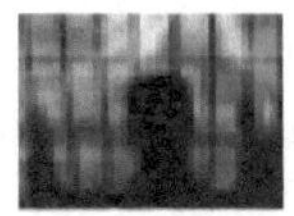

The heavy metal door slammed shut behind her, and the bolt slid across as if to emphasize that there was no way out. Only the dark silence of the cell to greet her.

So this was it, a cell measuring around twenty five foot by eighteen, four and a bit body lengths by three. Home for the foreseeable future. As her eyes adjusted to the light, Jean could see a bed at one end with a very grubby worn mattress, covered by a threadbare blanket. A jug and bowl lay in a corner beside a small stool, and in the other corner was a bucket. A small high window afforded some light, but once dark, there would be no electric light. Even in the unlikely event that the power was on, the bulb would have been smashed ages ago. That would be one trial to overcome, the coming of dusk, and acclimatisation to the gathering darkness.

Solitary confinement day one, hour one, minute three. How long would it be before she lost the count of days, and became so adjusted to her surroundings that full daylight, when she next saw it, would become too glaring, like standing in front of a spotlight. The mental erosion of incarceration would grind her down, or so they thought. Physical, mental, psychological separation from the outside world. No one to hear a cry of pain, or share a thought with. Even the birds outside avoided the place, due to its grim association with death and fear. Her stay could be five days or the full five years. Five years of staring at the same few square inches of wall, five years of fighting to keep focussed and not let them lead you out half mad into the light, to prove they had tamed you.

They would play all sorts of tricks on her – brutal, hard line regimes always did. You were 'forgotten about' for months on end. No one came to see you, your case appeared closed, your legal counsel dissuaded or physically prevented from visiting. No contact from loved ones either. Hope of getting out with an early hearing would evaporate. No small signs of encouragement anywhere. It was like walking a twenty metre tightrope between two cliffs. You feel totally on your own with no underlying support. One false move and you're finished.

For now it was time for bed, and she put down her small bag and lay on top of the blanket. This bed was filthy, and the blanket most likely inadequate once the night cold set in. Seasons meant little in this part of the world. It was always hot, sometimes very hot, and incessantly dry. At least the thick walls of the cell provided some respite from the heat. But night time was different. Then it got cold as the earth shed its heat, and she would have to sleep fully clothed. Perhaps in time she could persuade the guard to bring a second blanket in. But for now this thin blanket would be it. She thought about folding it in two, but that didn't provide complete cover for her body.

In the dark too, every sound was magnified. She heard some scurrying over the concrete floor, no doubt cockroaches creeping out of the cracks where floor joined wall. What hidden surprises would she uncover as the night wore on? In the distance she could hear the muezzin calling the faithful to prayer, a sound that would soon become familiar enough, and mark the time of day.

Holding an illegal meeting. That was the charge. A group of six women in her upper room had been meeting as part of an expat support group, while their menfolk were at work or away. They knew about the secret police and the need to be careful, in case they were being watched as foreigners. It was their second time meeting, and they had just started talking and sharing news when the police broke in, made arrests and took them away to a waiting van. Somebody must have observed and informed on them, but this was hardly subversive. When the rooms were searched, they found two Bibles, and used these as a pretext for accusing them of disrespect to Islam. Jean had tried to explain that they were just meeting together as friends and there was nothing religious involved, no prayer meeting or group Bible study, but the police would have none of it.

Then it was detention in an overcrowded cell, a quick trial and today's sentencing. Three years each with additional punishment of two more years for the leader, the time to be spent away from other inmates in solitary confinement. In reality she had just been hosting the meeting, but there always had to be a scapegoat.

The court had confused her, the judge almost shouting at the accused in a language she didn't understand. Her defence lawyer seemed weak. She had to find someone quick, taking a recommendation from a person she had once met. He was out of his depth arguing with this lot. The judge came down hard on him at every turn. The Bibles and other books taken from her rooms had been waved around as if evidence that she was a religious or political activist. She knew deep down they would make an example of her, but really examples were there to be seen, and in solitary she could be safely forgotten about. It was all a bit illogical. A trumped up charge from a regime paranoid about any perceived opposition.

Gradually as the light faded, she sought refuge in sleep. It had been a traumatic day, being escorted from the cells along with the other five, waiting in the court an age before proceedings started, and then hearing the sentences read out. There was no point in showing emotion. The whole situation was ridiculous. She had been a danger to no one, and at some point the stupidity of it all would be exposed. Then they had all been taken away, and driven for what seemed hours to the women's high security prison, Kedan, and in through two sets of huge iron gates into a yard. There they had been searched and issued the pale blue prison clothing. The others had left in a group, exchanging worried glances with her, while she was then led through a maze of corridors past the iron doors of cells and sound of their inmates, up stairs and then to this place at the far end of the passageway.

Somehow, you had to tune out and pretend it wasn't happening to you, to draw on an inner steel, to go deep inside yourself and show an expressionless mask to the outside world. If this was a nightmare come true, it had to be broken down into digestable chunks. The guards were unfriendly as if permanently stressed, pushing her needlessly through the door. These were the people who would control her life from now on and find any excuse to bring meals late and cold, speaking and acting harshly as if she was preventing them having an easy day.

Incarceration – a rare and unfriendly word with unpleasant overtones, like 'incineration.' Well that was now Jean's situation, a feeling of being entombed. While her friends would be let out a few times each day for exercise, the continuity of looking at murky plastered walls and a small patch of sky would be unbroken for her. There would be no 'take five' other than to shut your eyes and pretend you weren't here. No book to read or reread, and every sound heard would be a major event in the day, for in this wing silence reigned supreme. It would probably take a few days to sink in, if indeed they weren't herded up and taken somewhere else. Or more likely prepared for departure and then told it was cancelled, as every psychological trick would be played on them.

Eventually, listening to sounds was enough to send her to sleep, at last a chance to cut it all out. It couldn't really be happening to her could it? She had come here alone to teach English in an International School. It was a chance to earn some good money on a twelve month contract. In four weeks time she had been due to go back to UK and had no plans to return. The experience of living in Saudi Arabia had attracted her, as well as the opportunity to experience another side of teaching. Through contacts she had been able to rent two upper rooms where she stayed, and was able to take a daily taxi from there to the school, with her downstairs neighbour, Mark, also from England and teaching science at the same school. He had been out of the country at the time of the arrests. She had always been careful going outdoors, dressing modestly and only walking alone to the local market.

Apart from a brief moment when she woke in the early hours, Jean was able to sleep through. Somehow the sleep protected her from the horrendous experience of yesterday, building a wall that would enable her to handle the memory and move on. Perhaps 'move on' wasn't the right expression, as there was no moving anywhere from this cell. She woke to the friendliness of streaming sunlight, lighting the cell and enabled her to see the walls clearly for the first time. They were solid concrete, with little variation in texture and colour.

In one corner were the inscriptions of a previous inmate, written in a language she didn't understand. Maybe a cry for freedom, the fight of the human spirit against these four walls. She noticed a nail wedged between the edge of the floor and a wall. With care she extracted it, found herself a corner of blank wall and scratched her first stroke for day one, with the date and day, while she still remembered it: 24/9/05 a Thursday. Who knows in fifty days she wouldn't know what day of the week or date it was? It might be easy to miss one or two days marking the wall, once the mental stress took over. Besides, you didn't need to know the date here. There were no appointments or deadlines.

The guard brought a makeshift breakfast – a bowl of some kind of slurry that tasted foul and two crusts of bread. Despite her hunger, she ate little, and left most of the meal. More than anything she wanted to look out of the window. Standing on the bed gave her a restricted view of some buildings, but there was nothing that would give her a view to match the elevation of her cell. It was likely to be disappointing anyway, a view of unremitting grey from cell blocks and intervening yards, so perhaps leaving it to the imagination was best. Prisons were generally not bright or well maintained places.

For those who did think of escape there was the desert to contend with. Yesterday's long drive had not been for nothing, and served to show how isolated the prison was. The only way out was with friends on the outside. For the others in her group, with husbands to apply pressure, hire professional counsel, and seek an Appeal, there might be hope, but she doubted that would extend to her as a single woman. She was also sure that Mark, upon his return, would be strongly dissuaded from pleading her cause. However, she knew that he could be persistent.

In her high, remote location there would be little chance of anyone's steps approaching her cell. The guard removed her tray and bucket a few hours later, saying nothing in the process. She couldn't remember the last time she had said nothing to anyone all day. The gift of speech enabled us to communicate, but if we didn't have anyone to communicate with, did we need that gift? How strange would it feel to talk to someone after not talking for fifty days. She resolved to practice, to say out loud the numbers from one to a hundred, and every word that came into her head. To speak was to fight back against those who would break her, and she decided to make up her own raps to recite hour by hour:

'Light in my cell is light in my life,

With room to perform, I'm sharp as a knife.'

Physical exercise had the same affect. She stretched and tensed her muscles, spread the blanket over the floor and did ten press ups, then lay on her back and pulled her upper body forward to meet her feet. To stay sane was to stay fit. To stay fit was to stay confident, believe in yourself and keep the darkness away.

An essential key for survival was music. Singing aloud every song that she had learnt as a young girl at school or humming her favourite pop tunes. Words that she hadn't sung for years being retrieved from the archives of memory and practiced until perfect. She would sit at a pretend piano and play tunes from memory. Concerts were prepared and recited to an imaginary audience. Every detail was observed from walking on stage, taking a bow and receiving a bouquet of pretend flowers, to waiting for the orchestra or sitting at the piano stool. Jean had never been a choral singer but now made herself rehearse selected songs again and again until they came naturally. Each day she delivered a ten item matinee and evening performance, taking pride in introducing new pieces, and making up lyrics where she had forgotten them.

Stretching and stimulating the mind was the real struggle. The invitation this place offered was to give up, to lie on the bed all day in a semi-comatosed state, mind switched off, and let the hours drift by. Jean was determined to fight, to give herself a series of mental challenges, be it identifying all the prime numbers between 1 and 501 or trying to make as many words as possible out of a random group of seven letters: five consonants and two vowels. With V,B,Y,P,L,O,I, how many four letter words could she make? Ten would be good, twenty almost impossible, and fifteen a good compromise. All she lacked was pencil and paper.

Then there was the fight to retain memory. Jean made herself remember as much as she could about what she had done in the last month, hour by hour and day by day. Recollection tested every link in the mind, every thought association. Once tapped, it led easily on to other thoughts on other days, like finding a vein of gold in a rock. The labyrinth of rediscovery. Losing memory of what happened on a morning or afternoon was like losing part of yourself. The battle to recall was a victory for self esteem.

The phases of the day were long as the unrelenting sun moved round the sky. Jean reflected on the fact that she was in one way better off on her own. Saudi prisons were notoriously overcrowded, and she felt that others may well be sharing cells, living in close proximity with strangers. Her space wasn't big - six paces by four, but it was hers and no one could take it away. She began to get to know it intimately, each shade of the grey wall and each bubble in an otherwise smooth floor surface.

However, the food was getting to her – an unvaried bland diet, that was, at times, difficult to digest. She couldn't afford to get ill here, and so forced herself to eat, though the morning slurry made her sick at first. Hunger was hard to fight, especially at night. The female guards were not receptive to requested changes or larger portions. Water was the only drink, tasting foul and again making her ill but better than nothing. She felt herself losing weight.

Day 25

They say mental deterioration can occur within weeks in solitary confinement, and Jean was now entering her fourth week alone. So far she was winning the battle, but you had to stay strong every moment of the day, and never weaken. There was something about the act of waiting that meant there was an end in sight. You waited for the doctor knowing that within thirty minutes, you would be seen. If she had hope in an early release, then she could believe she was waiting for that, but as the days rolled past, it was increasingly difficult to believe that that would happen. There was really nothing to wait for, but to realise that was to admit defeat. Keeping the flame of faith going was everything. By its very existence, the Kedan prison destroyed hope and faith. Even those who got out on early release were often already broken, the mental and psychological damage complete.

Part of Jean's role play was to believe she would be released in two hours, to mentally tune herself to what she would do when re-entering the world, who she would see, and where she would go. She thought sometimes about the school and the disruption to her students, who had been about to sit exams. What would this have done to her reputation? Make her sound like an irresponsible adult, or did they know her well enough to understand the injustice of it? You couldn't be sure. Once released, she would leave Saudi immediately. Get the first plane home. There would be friends in UK who would have expected to hear from her. Her eighty year old mother too. What would they be thinking now. Had Mark taken any steps to raise her case with the Consulate? She might never know. Interference with local justice could get him into trouble too.

Cling on to that hope, just cling on.

Day 47

Six weeks and five days had passed. Jean was faithful in recording a scratch for each day, and so presumed today was Tuesday November 10th. Normally you would tell the days of the week by the different activities. Sunday would be a quiet day back home. Friday was the key difference out here, and you could still detect that by listening. Apart from that every day was the same, and weekdays meant nothing.

She must have lost at least a stone – physical strength was ebbing faster than mental. She could control her mind, but her body needed more food, more vitamins. The exercises were getting shorter and harder, and periods of resting on the bed, longer. Her only visitor was always a female guard, usually two different guards who rotated shifts, and rarely spoke a word. She had tried talking to them to get a response but was sure they were under instruction to never reply. All part of the mental erosion. Engaging in dialogue was a form of offering humanity and hope.

It was tempting to get more desperate about release, the more hopeless it became, but she was not there yet. Jean was good at controlling her emotions. She hadn't cried or sobbed yet. They would not break her.

Day 71

Now ten weeks in solitary. You could start to hallucinate, to go mad or you could dig deep and survive. The mind and body were weaker. Hunger and nausea were common, eating more difficult. Every mental exercise had been practised, but she was clinging on. If Jean had a pencil and book, she would have kept a diary. Instead it was all compartmentalised in the mind. Awaking each morning after fitful sleep still gave her hope, but she could feel herself slipping.

Day 99

Over fourteen weeks now. Three months. Probably it was around Christmas. She was barely moving off the bed. Physical movement was tiring and her exercises much reduced. But still, she had the key to her mind. She would never surrender that.

The sound of footsteps in the corridor, no she must be imagining it. They never came here. Must be the guards again.

The key turned and the door swung open.

'Jean Woods? 1894853?'

She slowly turned round

'Yes?'

'Peter Evans from the British Consulate.'

He smiled at her. She responded weakly.

'A number of people have been campaigning for your release. I'm pleased to say that the Court has reviewed your case and will release you later today. But you should leave the country straight away.'

She opened her eyes wide, scarcely believing him.

'Really?'

'Yes, we've been working hard on your behalf. The original evidence against you was questionable. The others in your group were released a few weeks ago. In your case it was harder.'

He went on. 'You will need to be medically checked and a car will take you to the airport. I suggest you don't go home first. We have issued a ticket and replacement passport.'

It was taking time to sink in. The precious gift of freedom. An hour ago so far away, but now within reach. The role play had not been in vain.

A Real Story

'Story, Daddy, story.'

Stuart was half way there, waiting like the orchestra's encore for a bit more pressure to be applied. His half smile was full of invitation. Ask and keep asking.

'Oh I don't know, it's getting late and it's a big day tomorrow,' he replied, putting up token resistance.

'You say that every time. Every day is a big day. I want a story or I won't go to sleep.'

Karen his daughter was just seven years old, an only child. Putting her to bed was a Daddy treat after June, her mother, had bathed or showered her. Reading one of her many library books was the norm when time was short and she was tired, but sometimes it needed something more, a story made up by her Dad, running out to three or four instalments, each reserved for that special twenty minutes between going to bed and lights out. Stuart could hardly remember the plots and themes he had pulled out of his imagination, but each was carefully recollected by his daughter for whom the characters resonated with a reality of their own.

'Can I have another Dorothy Eggles?'

'I think Dorothy is away to see her mum, darling.' Stuart felt she had been done to death.

'Oh well Professor Fantos then. He's always here.'

Another well known character whose crazy inventions had put Karen into fits of laughter many times. The rotating car had been a huge hit.

'But Professors need time for their next brainwave. I think he'll be too busy.'

'Well you decide STORY!'

Stuart hadn't finished yet, evasiveness giving way to teasing.

'You have to lie still for two minutes while I think. Daddy has to search his memory for something,' he said, making it sound like a visit to the library archives.

Karen made a distinction between stories and real stories. Stories were understood to be fictional, made up characters and a plot, such as you read in many children's books. Like a big furry cat having nocturnal adventures as it ran over tiled roofs. Real stories, however, were stories based on something that actually happened. Somewhere, possibly at the start or buried in the middle was a core of fact, a real person, a real experience, but it was enveloped in fiction. A find of old coins buried for centuries led to a story of how they had come to be left there. Karen would often ask if the story she was about to hear was a 'real story', sometimes seemingly disappointed if it wasn't.

The pause was no longer than thirty seconds.

'Hurry up Daddy I want a real story tonight.'

'OK, ok.'

Lying on the bed, Stuart made himself more comfortable, thinking of a way to start. Most of his bedtime stories were like driving a car in thick fog – you hadn't a clue where you were going. Plot, theme and everything else evolved as you went along. Two characters were enough to begin.

'Close your eyes and imagine a big old house, much bigger than ours, with three floors, big staircases, and lots of rooms. It has its own grounds with trees, flower beds, and a big vegetable garden.'

'Is it bigger than the palace where the Queen lives?'

'Well not quite… but it's very big, and four children live there, two boys and two girls. They have lots of rooms to play and keep their toys in.'

'Oooh what are their names?'

Stuart was good at pulling names out of the air, but had been caught out a few times in mis-remembering them, so that Clare had become Clarissa by the next evening, only to be promptly and correctly renamed.

'Well, this is a Victorian household from over one hundred years ago, so the boys were called Gordon and Trevor and the girls, Penny and Josephine. Do you like those names?'

'Yes, they're good.'

Just as well since they weren't up for negotiation. You could only be interactive so much.

'Gordon is the eldest – he's thirteen years old, then Penny, the eldest girl, is nine years old. She's got long blonde hair tied at the back, blue eyes and a big smile. The children play in rooms on the second floor, one of which has a big doll's house that Penny loves to play with.'

'Is it bigger than mine?'

'Oh yes,' said Stuart, remembering the big Victorian dolls houses he had seen. He went on to describe each room, including the basement rooms used by the household staff. The fascination of detail, down to the toy mirrors, clocks on the mantelpiece, and candelabra on the tables. This was a forgotten private world where each ornate room had its function and name – the Drawing Room, Dining Room, Study, children's Nursery, each properly furnished, and with watercolours or early framed photos on each wall. The strong sense of order and purpose, feeling proper rather than powerful, contrasted with today's compact modern houses with more modest interiors.

In the remaining time, he tried to convey that to Karen, giving her a glimpse of a bygone age, and letting her imagination take over. There was something rather haunting about it. People who walked the same streets as you or I, but one hundred and fifty years ago, thinking things and living lives that were so alien to what we know today. Our society has re-invented itself probably two or three times over since then, from the strongly affirmed Victorians to the uncertainties of the two World Wars that changed the whole fabric of society, before re-emerging in the optimism of the 60s and 70s. How quickly things had changed even within Stuart's own lifetime. Twenty years ago we knew nothing of wireless internet, mobile phones, social media, skype, carbon footprint. Maybe we are now re-inventing ourselves on a 10-15 year cycle that was once a 50 year cycle last century. Will 2035 man or woman recognise who they once were in 2012? Quite a thought.

Karen's eyes grew heavy and soon she was asleep, leaving Stuart to gently extricate his arm and lever himself off the bed. He stood for a moment as if transfixed, unwilling to proceed with the rest of his evening, but soon turned and walked downstairs. He made himself a cup of tea, and prepared the laptop for some items he needed to order online. What would the father of his Victorian mansion have done? Written a list with his best ink fountain pen to pass to the housekeeper, who would see that one of the boys ran down into the town the following morning to get the requested items, if indeed they could be obtained locally.

A real story, based on the lives of a wealthy Victorian family, or was it? Did they live as we imagined them to, as disciplined, obedient children often seeing more of their governess than their mother, or were there cracks in the facade, tensions, dissension, discontent. An absentee father leaving his wife to run the household, mind the children, organise the household staff, effectively lead while he was frequently away on business. A home with unhappy undercurrents. The intervening century and a half allows us to see them, but not hear them, to assume that the pattern of their lives occurred in the way they wanted it to occur, that they, not other circumstances, were in control.

Stuart had little time for the local free paper. Ongoing battles over council spending cuts held little appeal, and so he quickly scanned the front page, intending to consign it to the bin. After that he went over to the laptop, googled some websites and started to investigate purchasing a new stereo system. Over the next hour he narrowed his choices, but decided to sleep on his intended purchase overnight. Never do anything major late in the day. Drinking some more tea, he watched some TV and then went up to bed.

He lay awake for an hour, his mind running over his day. Uneventful at work, a quiet weekend ahead, there was little remarkable happening. This was February, a seemingly dull month, when the fatigue of a long winter had not yet given way to the promise of spring. Strong winds and rain were forecast. Evenings were getting lighter but it was still cold out there. He would have liked to fast forward his life to Easter, with a holiday break in the spring sunshine, but that was still some weeks away. The only plan at present was not to have a plan, to take each day as it came.

Next day, waking to the sound of rain, Stuart showered and headed for work. Returning that evening, he helped Karen with her reading, and then came bedtime. He didn't need to think about the story. She had remembered it perfectly, so without further need for encouragement, Stuart resumed.

In his mind was an old mansion on a hill nearby. It had become a private hospital, but had been closed for years. It had four floors, with a long front to the circular driveway and two wings going back into the estate. Rooms that had once been full of conversation, laughter and action, were now empty, abandoned. Their story had run its course over eighty years. Lawns that had seen garden parties, trails through the woods worn with the footsteps of guests, long dining tables with fourteen seated for dinner, and fireplaces where logs had crackled as board or card games were played. Gentlemen filling their pipes, enjoying a whisky and talking for hours. Ladies in conversation over tea in the Drawing Room. A buzz that resonated, growing to a crescendo, but gradually dying. A story that might never be told.

The council had decided after much deliberation to pull it down last year, and so the contractors moved in and the place was reduced to rubble. It was built in the affirmation and belief that it would last hundreds of years, but was demolished in days, with no one even shedding a tear.

'The family were called Harbell. Mr Harbell worked as a solicitor in London. He took a pony and trap to the station each morning but was away long hours, and often slept in a flat above his office. But he was home each weekend. So Mrs Harbell had the responsibility of making sure everything ran well. She had to make sure there was enough money for the food, pay the housekeeper, cook, gardener and two maids, and of course look after four growing children.'

'Did they have to go to school?'

'Yes, but not as much as you do. Only when they were older. A tutor used to come to the house to teach the children, so one of the first floor rooms was a school room with tables and books. Gordon, the eldest boy, was already at boarding school in the country but came home for holidays.'

'Wow, a tutor. Sounds better than having to go to school.'

'Yes, but you'd miss your friends. Besides, the tutor made them work hard because they were fewer. Your teacher has thirty children to worry about, their tutor only had three.'

'Yes, I suppose so. Did they each have their own bedroom?'

'They do now. The two girls being the youngest had the same room until Penny was seven. The rooms are all next to each other on the first floor. Trevor has the biggest.'

'What did they eat?'

'Same as what you and I eat, but food was fresh. There were no refrigerators. They would have set mealtimes, like dinner at six o'clock. There was a big grandfather clock in the hall so everyone knew when it struck six. Cook would prepare a three course meal – soup, main course and dessert. Mother and Father sat at either end of the table with the children on each side. On weekends they would have guests to dinner, family friends or relatives. Aunt Daisy would come up from the New Forest to stay sometimes.'

'I bet they had a big garden for hide and seek.'

'Yes, they had lawns and a small area of woods. All those trees to hide behind! Mother told them that the vegetable garden and flowerbeds were out of bounds for games. The grounds had a high wall, so they couldn't get lost, and there were big gates at the front. Imagine how you would feel to have so much space to play in.'

'What toys did they have?'

'Well we spoke about the Doll's House. The girls also had a rocking horse, dolls, and teddy bears. The boys had model trains.'

And so the picture evolved – the sanctity of the home, a busy healthy place in its own universe, the outside world delivering everything and everyone to its doorstep, from potatoes to coal, piano teachers to brass cleaners. A nineteeth century world pre-bicycle and car, with transport by horse and carriage into the local town. A world with formal gardens, hedgerows, greenhouse, manicured lawns, sectioned space. A world before television, with guests arriving for the evening, long involved discussions over dinner, drinks and formal entertainment with singing, violin and piano. A world of children kept away from adults, bathed and put to bed early by the governess, who read them the classics of their era. This was the high noon of Victorian Britain, the 1860s.

For Karen it was all so strange, a painted scene observed from a distance. Beautiful on the one hand but also rather unreal. Life on a grand scale but strangely limited at the same time. She yawned and was soon asleep again, the day consigned to past memory.

Stuart had lifted the lid. The effect of telling was to discover how much more there was to tell, his task for the next few evenings. It was as if each room in the house needed to be unlocked and viewed, its contents adding something new to our understanding of the idea of home, and what it means to enter its domestic world. And importantly this was not our own home, which wouldn't interest us, but the fascination of how someone else lived in their private world. How they created a mini-society, how they decorated and furnished the huge spaces they owned, who they shared it with, what happiness it gave them, and how it reflected their values. In short, how they managed their bubble.

But perhaps the real moment was one that you couldn't tell to a child, one that prompted explanation, but needed none, on the rare occasions that it happened. When the children were away, Mrs Harbell would sit alone and play the 'Moonlight Sonata' on the grand piano, each chord swelling in volume as the legato tune reached both high and then low notes. As the tears rolled down her face, it spoke of released emotions, expression, the need to speak for the soul of this castle, the radiance of light and music echoing to its every corner, scattering its dark secrets, opening its hidden doors, and exposing it to the rawness of human emotion.

The sobbing grew in chorus to the piano, as if fuelling the performance. Sobbing for a happiness that can never be realised, despite the ostentatious wealth of this home, for an unfulfilled life that yearned for something better. Sobbing for the pain of children that every parent feels responsible for. But this was not a cry for help, nor a cry of desperation. It was a plea for the captive spirit, caught in a web of expectation, false smiles, lonely evenings, rigid timetables, suffocating politeness, worries over children and staff. Like a wolf howling in the moonlight, it chose its moment and came forth. As twilight became darkness, the sound appeared to grow, defying light to disappear, challenging the demons of the night, and anaesthetising the pain of life with a moment of beauty.

She played fluently, like a butterfly fluttering for the first time, flapping its new wings. This required no score, it flowed from the heart, pouring out into space. The key changed, the chords moved up an octave in a crescendo, then down again for the ensuing diminuendo, but the tune never wavered. She knew it intimately from years of experience, played the first movement to its finish, and then started again.

This was her anthem, the story of her life, a piece of music played in the light of a full moon, yet symbolising her struggles and triumphs, joys and sorrows, loves and fears. The repetition in the tune allowed her to say and say again her message, a cry of loneliness, and strength, but never a call of sadness or defeat. The haunting melody was hers. She was at this moment without mask or facade, her true self, both calling out to the world, and gaining comfort in so doing. The music was cathartic, both releasing the emotions that she did so well to hide and absorbing the joy of expression. It empowered her – she could now survive the regimentation of the household, once again be seen to be strong. Yet no one must see her play, no one see the tears. They were for her alone, her visit to her private garden.

The fifth time through, she played the final chords and finished. She had spoken to this great house, which she would never leave or be allowed to leave. The silence spoke volumes, as if the walls themselves paid tribute. Slowly she rose from the stool and walked to the door. Soon she must light the lamps and greet the returning children, but first she wiped her face and sat alone transfixed on the couch, observing the final seconds of this special time, this secret she shared with her silent fortress.

Parting

'We've got three quarters of an hour, so we may as well grab a cup of tea.'

'OK, but it looks a bit crowded over in "Tessa's". Might have to do a take away instead. We can sit over there.'

'Tell you what, you take those seats and I'll queue. Tea for you Clare, and what about you, son?'

Bob, as ever, took charge of the situation, his decisiveness overcoming the nerves that were setting in. He dumped the heavy case by a set of three metal seats.

'Oh I dunno. Maybe a bottle of sparkling water.'

Bob and Clare Evans were at Kings Cross station to see their son James off for his first term at University.

The train for Newcastle would depart promptly at 3pm, and it would be good to secure a window seat for him beforehand. But for now the platform was empty, and an awkward wait would have to be filled before the incoming train arrived. The ever efficient Bob was soon back with the drinks.

'There you are dear, two sugars. One of these lollipop sticks to stir with.'

They sat cramped, yet fortunate to be able to sit, while the bustle of a mainline station carried on around them. A final whistle for the train departing platform 8 shrieked, as two women dashed to the last open carriage door. Trains had a certain finality about them, and, while much maligned, waited for no one. The echoing announcements proceeded, ignored by many. Long queues waited at ticket machines to do the necessary. A noisy group of arrivals from the Edinburgh train were making their way to one of several underground entrances. The whole place was a shrine to movement – to and from trains, station exits, taxi ranks, lunch appointments. In a place where it was so easy to look confused, it was important not to be. You came through here to somewhere, the true definition of being in transit. Any movement was purposeful. He or she who hesitated was lost.

'You'll be fine son. You'll have the time of your life.'

'You must have said that ten times,' commented Clare to her husband.

'All right, but he will.' Bob insisted. 'They have all sorts of clubs – theatre, choir, full range of sports.'

He was speaking to some extent in ignorance, but wanting to be the optimist. Somehow he saw it as his role to try and brighten the wait, fill the time.

James just nodded out of politeness, and checked his phone as much to see the time as for messages, thus avoiding the impoliteness of checking his watch. Time was crawling past. Still over thirty five minutes to departure. He took another sip of water.

'You will remember to ring when you arrive?' Clare asked him.

'Yes mum.'

'How will they get you to the halls of residence?' inquired Bob.

'There's a bus from the station. The train will be full of first years.'

'Is that what they call Freshers or Freshmen?' asked Bob after a pause, each lull in the conversation seeming too uncomfortable to tolerate.

'Freshers, Dad. Freshmen is US.'

'What time will you get up there?'

'Journey time is three hours to the station and then it's around thirty minutes. Should be there by seven o'clock.' James reassured them.

'Oh that's not too bad. Thought it might be longer. Sounds like a fast journey.' Bob was reassured.

He paused, unsure of what to say next.

'This time in two days you won't know yourself.' Bob's continued optimism irritated his son, more by his fighting the silence than the inane comments he made.

'Oh, did you pack any mugs?' Clare seemed startled at her own question.

'Yes mum, set of four. It's Ok.'

The case had been checked several times in addition to the trunk he had packed for collection. It was as if his whole life was being packed away – kitchenware, books, PC notebook, DVDs, bed linen, sleeping bag, sports kit, lamps, clothing, posters, and of course his prize possession, his Playstation. Painstakingly everything has been assembled sorted, discarded, rearranged, packed and finally repacked till there was not a spare cubic centimetre of space in either the massive trunk or his suitcase. Somewhere in the middle of all that were the four mugs packed around clean socks and tee shirts. It had taken hours, with no shortage of parental advice. James, ever the outdoors type, had insisted on including his tent despite the space it took up, making the task even harder.

It had been the first step in the process of leaving home. An assertion of independence, perhaps the first of many. They had all been overjoyed the day he got his place at Newcastle University, remembering what a tough interview he had undergone. And who knew where this would lead, when he would return home and on what basis. For all the talk of high rents around London, students having to pay off loans, and the likelihood of staying at home till his mid twenties, James was less certain of returning. Ever one to break the mould, he saw any coming back home as only temporary. University would open his eyes, widen his horizons, and propel him in the direction of different places, even overseas. If volunteers for a South American field trip in the vacation were called for, his hand would be the first to be raised.

For Clare, this was an inevitable bittersweet moment that marked the next stage of life. A son she had nurtured over eighteen years, a maturing teenager, was now ready to go out into the world. Of course, she was happy that he had got his place to read Geology. It was his passion and he would thrive in the academic environment of a university. They had all visited Newcastle and liked the city and student accommodation but his parting left a hole in her life. No son to get up for breakfast, to hear talking about life, friends, the world, always something stimulating. He had been away for short periods before to scout camp, and for holidays with friends, but this was the first real departure. The house would be quiet without him, weekends that bit more dull and lifeless. He was their only child.

Bob would throw himself into golf, the football club and manage to carry on, but she would feel the loss more. Yes James would be home for Christmas, in three months, but it was never the same. His life, mannerisms, chat, and laughter would have moved on away from the family nest. He would still be recognisable, but would now have become a young man. By the time the next term started in January, he would already have changed, and the farewells then would be much more low key.

Life is a series of meetings – a handshake for an introduction. Meet a new person. Some just held out a limp hand, others embraced yours and looked you in the eye, appreciating the significance of the moment. The start of an association that might last hours or even decades. 'Do you remember when we first met?' The meeting itself was perhaps less important than what followed. The formality that opened the gate to a social, professional, or even marital friendship or partnership. Many of them would never have an ending, a kiss or handshake of farewell. Sometimes the formality of parting resulted in meeting the person again sooner than expected, as if the final handshake were unnecessary. Conversely, the absence of that farewell recognition was often associated with never seeing that person again, an oversight always regretted. A person to whom you never said goodbye, and now could never do so.

Increasingly, the continuity of life meant that we could skip introductions, and just get straight on with relating, while forgetting about farewells because we never wanted to recognise an ending, forever hoping there was more to come. Yet somehow the moments of starting and ending still carry a significance that we are loathe to lose, and will remember for a long time. They are like running the one hundred metre race, with lots of build up and meaning, but over in seconds.

For the Evans family now, it seemed like an interminable wait. Each sat in their own world for a few minutes. Even Bob was stunned into silence. Random thoughts came and went, as none of them could concentrate on anything. Best just to sip your drink and observe the world passing by, enjoy its unique pattern of people, luggage, conversations, movement and of course, the pigeons. Yes, there were always pigeons in every London station, perching in the rafters and swooping to fight over a half eaten bread roll, unafraid of the humanity close by.

As Bob looked up the inbound express had pulled in and passengers piled out. It was time to get on and find a good seat. Bob lifted the big case, and they all walked over to the platform, noticing a gathering crowd, similar to themselves. Parents, that had come to see their sons and daughters off.

'Whatever you've got in here weighs a ton!' gasped Bob as they walked along the platform to the second class compartments, getting in at the first available carriage. Seats were already occupied, but they soon found one and lifted the case onto the rack.

'There, a nice seat with a window view. Three hours to daydream.'

James ignored his father's comment, and his parents now stood awkwardly in the passageway being politely asked to move by other passengers. There was a further twenty minutes to go before departure.

'Don't forget the snack box. Salad sandwiches in the blue lid, and fruit and yoghurt in the green.' Clare had prepared his meal meticulously including a small jar of olives that he was so fond of.

'Yes mum, seen them.'

'They'll give you dinner when you arrive I expect.'

'Yeah, there's something in the letter about that.' James didn't seem too concerned.

'Stick your rucksack down on the seat, and come out to the platform,' said Bob.

They walked to the carriage doorway and stood on the platform. This was it.

'Well son…' Bob was lost for words. The poignancy of a moment they had uneasily waited for had finally come. Their only child leaving home for the first time. This was hardly a troop train heading for an uncertain war, but each parting had its pain. Necessary, quick, dreaded, but so important. A brief marker in time and life.

Clare had started crying and put a tissue to her eyes.

'Wishing you the very best, son. Have a great time. I'm sure you will. Let us know.' Bob embraced his son in a tight hug, his sentence trailing away.

Clare kissed James on the cheek, tears streaming down her face.

'Goodbye my baby boy,' she mumbled.

James swallowed, wiping away a tear, and turned quickly as if not wanting to prolong the emotion. He returned to his seat in what was now a full carriage. It was done. Time now to look forward.

'Let's go, it's hard enough for him,' Bob whispered softly, as he put his arm around Clare. They could have lingered outside the carriage window, but decided to walk away and return just before the train departed. They waited numbly at the end of the platform.

Their self absorption could have lasted hours. There was nothing to say, just memories of a crawling child who grew into a happy teenager, now ready to grow again. It symbolised the inherent conflict of life, progress versus stability. Somehow, when you grew older, and when you could handle progress better, all you wanted was stability – the same home, job, habits, faces. As if somehow the change of youth into twenties and thirties had seen enough of change. When you were young it was the opposite, less experience with handling progress combined with a constant diet of it. Transience - living two years here, a year there and moving on in life to the next place. Happy to embrace and absorb the turns on the path.

The station clock stood at two minutes to three o'clock, and so they walked slowly up to the carriage. Bob rapped on the window, and pulled a face. James smiled and waved. The doors slammed, and they both waved back as the train slowly pulled off.

'Come on love, let's head home. That's him away.'

They gazed at the train till it disappeared from view, then turned to make their way home. The silence did all the talking.

Sunny Spells

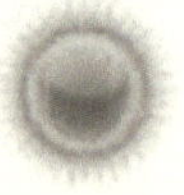

The force of the March wind nearly blew him off his feet as he reached the top of the hill. He had been glad that it wasn't raining when he left the house, but the weather now had other surprises in store. While high winds had been forecast, Bill somehow didn't think they would arrive so soon, or maybe he just didn't think. He found that the weather was one of those things that was always present, day and night, so that he often didn't focus on it. It was something you couldn't control, but something that rarely limited what you wanted to do. Visits to friends, shops, schools, offices, even resorts carried on regardless, except in the extreme conditions of icy roads, or hurricane winds. Nevertheless, the weather must be the greatest conversation topic, the best ice breaker for awkward moments with strangers:

'Nice day today.'

'Yes, isn't it. What a beautiful morning! It's expected to cloud over this afternoon though.'

Imagine the alternative, how would you chat to your neighbour if we had no weather, or if it was always the same?

'Good breakfast?'

'Yes, two toast and jam. And you?'

Strange perhaps, but we would always find something to talk about, some accepted universal topic that invited our view or observation. The weather was safe because no one felt threatened at its mention, and truly, at times of warm sunshine or torrential rain, it was worthy of discussion. There could also be no doubting its effect on the national psyche– sunny days lifting the gloom, rainy ones bringing it back.

Then there was that other aspect of weather, the forecast. Weather wasn't just for now, what it was doing in the present, the weather of the next few days was of huge interest. Everyone knows the forecast, so easily accessible on radio and TV, and relishes the prospect of an unseasonally sunny weekend in early spring or the likelihood of the first winter snowfalls. Maybe the sheer changeability of it made for such fascination, the unpredictability of the weather matching the unpredictability of life. The sunny spells of the good times – safe job, happy holidays, new daughter or son in law, giving way suddenly to rain showers – ill health, a car accident, falling share prices.

Sometimes they were in harmony, life's peaks coinciding with sunny days, but often they were out of synch with each other - like sitting on a park bench on a hot June day, stunned by bad news, or feeling like dancing with happiness in the rain. The venerated barometer in the hallway could perhaps instead measure our lives – the low pressure of illness or bad exam results, and the high pressure of success.

The scarf Bill had put away two weeks ago, during a brief sunny spell, was suddenly necessary with the drop in temperature. Right now, it felt like five degrees colder with the wind chill, and the cold got into your bones. It made the 16 degree normal temperature for March seem warm. At least he still wore his gloves and woollen hat, usually pushed well into his pockets until weeks after their last seasonal use.

The forty minute mid-morning walk with the dog, round the edge of the town and up onto the downs, was a habit from which he never deviated regardless of the weather. Come rain or shine, he attached a lead to the collar of Tracy, their black Labrador, put on his walking shoes, and headed through the maze of streets to the footpath over the fields and into the woods. There was a certain beauty in the daily repetition – it had become a pillar round which to base the other activities of the day, and a litmus test to check what was going on in the world. In the last five years, since he retired from work, Bill had only missed a handful of days.

How could weather be classed as bad? This was a question he had often asked himself. Weather was weather, inanimate, with no bias or statement to make. The general view was that rain meant bad weather, but in many parts of the world, rain was welcomed as the start of the wet season. Rain was good, it meant that crops would grow and there would be plenty to go round. The continued drought from hot sunny days, by contrast, spelt economic disaster. Perhaps 'good' and 'bad' had to be dropped, but they were well embedded in the national psyche.

In life too, a seemingly bad event like losing a job, can become the 'best thing that ever happened to me.' Once pushed out of a role and forced to find a different one, many never looked back. Yet no one would deny that being involved in a car accident as either cause or victim was anything other than a bad thing, just as a force eight gale rarely did anyone any good. Where was the boundary, what was the difference?

And then there were the extremes – tornadoes and hurricanes that devastated tropical communities, tearing roofs off homes, tossing cars around like confetti. Their impact was severe, lasting hours but with damage that would take years to rebuild, and lives that would have to start over again. It was difficult to think of a positive equivalent – good weather by definition is gentle, smooth, stable, but hardly extreme. Not what you would call 'ecstatic'.

Bill pondered many of these things on his morning constitutional. He was active for his age and in good health. He rarely got ill - in fact he believed his daily ritual was an anaesthetic against it. The best way to combat a cold, he felt, was to take a walk in cold weather wearing a thick coat, not hide away from it. The ascent to the hill too, where he now stood, kept him fit, thus defying the aging process. It had become a way of affirming his love of life, of being in the moment.

One of his favourite sayings was 'assume nothing.' His wife Jeanette had first heard it with discomfort as it somehow undermined the security she sought. Yet after the sudden death of her sister, a stock market crash that had wiped away half the value of their pensions, and the worst town floods for eighty years, she had begun to realise what he meant. We all want life to change, which is what makes it interesting, but somehow expect that to happen within certain boundaries that carry forward everything and everybody we love in its path. Yet nothing is inevitable or certain, and sometimes it took a shock to understand that. Bill was adaptable, he could live within his means and manage without the new car he had promised himself. They had already paid off their home, and had inexpensive tastes. A lower than expected pension was therefore no disaster. His two children were well into their twenties and their careers - healthy signs.

He braved the strength of the wind, holding on to his hat, and began the slow walk down to the lane that ran through a gully, sheltered from the gusts. The daffodils in the bank alongside were starting to flower, showing an array of colour that had been absent a few days ago, part of the never failing cycle of nature that offered signs of hope in the midst of harsh and bitter weather. Spring, Easter, longer evenings leading into May, and some warmth. It was all ahead of them. This was the promise of spring indeed even if reality was different – overcast, cool, wet and so on. We look forward with great interest to the coming of spring, but rarely look back to reflect on the fulfilment of the promise. Did we get what we thought we would? By then we're into summer and looking forward to something else.

As he returned to the house, he spotted his neighbour Mr. Jeffries in his drive.

'Cold today – bitter in that wind,' Bill greeted.

'You can't trust the weather. A few mild days and it gets cold again.'

Like so many comments on the weather people make, it was glaringly obvious, but somehow a common feeling they both shared made it not only acceptable but also perceptive.

'Almost blew me away on top of Bennetts Hill,' continued Bill. 'I'll be glad to get in and have a cup of hot coffee. Won't be going too far in this.'

'Indeed.'

Not wanting to linger, Bill went to his front porch, put the key in the lock and walked in. The warmth from the central heating hit him immediately. As expected there was a pile of mail to open and the daily paper to peruse.

'You must be frozen.' Jeanette boiled the jug for morning coffee.

'Yes, it's not pleasant at all out there,' he commented.

'Well get yourself warm and drink this.' She poured his coffee, put some biscuits on a plate and returned to the kitchen.

Bill opened the paper. A small paragraph on the front page told him that it had been the coldest February for twenty five years. He wasn't surprised, at times it had barely been above zero. So many weather observations were like this, backed by statistical analysis. A mass of recorded facts and readings sifted into a pattern that provided proof and support for our instinctive feelings. A statistician's paradise! Averages that hide the fact that no two Februaries would ever have the same weather. We should get an average temperature of 'x', but in 2013, we got 'y', two degrees colder. The year of the really cold February, reflected Bill. How we analyse everything from the weather to the stock market and the football results!

Yet strangely it stopped where it affected ourselves, he observed. We don't like to be reminded that we overspent last month or failed to do something we normally do. Feelings without facts were enough. We don't care to analyse ourselves too much, maybe just preferring to have a rough idea that things are going well or badly. We have that vague hunch that we should have spent more time with the family, but don't want to be told how few hours we were actually together. Looking at your finances too closely too often might be worrying or uncomfortable. And as for the unexpected, no one ever predicts getting the sack. Yet everyone loves to analyse something. The weather was just one more thing, its behaviour compartmentalised and compared, its indices up and down.

Bill had a fascination with meteorology. He had had a Stevenson screen erected in the garden to measure temperature and wind, as well as a separate rain gauge. The readings went back ten years. His pet subject was global warming, but discerning weather patterns over the last few years wasn't easy. Two cool summers had been followed by a record hot summer last year, and then wild winter storms with flooding. While this was seen as support for global warming, Bill still remained sceptical. How much extreme weather would have happened anyway, regardless of artificial warming? Yes, the jet steams had moved and that caused wind systems to shift location, but was the destruction of the ozone layer really responsible? The case was unproven in his eyes. It was too easy to scapegoat global warming.

He flicked quickly through the newspaper, and then turned to the pile of unopened mail, using a knife to open six envelopes. The gas bill held few surprises, likewise the bank statement. It still amazed him that companies still sent advertising through the mail, given the ease and cost efficiency of email, so two of his letters were torn into pieces and disposed. That done, he turned on his laptop to check email and his online bank accounts, another part of his daily routine. Then he would go out to the garden, read the instruments and rain gauge, and record the readings on his spreadsheet. At least he wasn't spending his retirement fussing over share prices. Running a weekly lunchtime club for pensioners, which he still did as a Lions Club committee member, was a far more valuable activity.

His morning routine led up to lunchtime, and he was soon chatting to Jeanette over the fish she had so carefully prepared.

'It'd take a hurricane to prevent you walking Tracy,' she remarked, knowing how incorrigible her husband was.

Bill was a hundred miles away, linking 'hurricane' and 'Tracy' into 'Hurricane Tracy'. He quickly resurfaced, realising what she had said.

'Yes, yes we always go. Can't allow the weather to stop that.'

'I was going to head for the shops this afternoon, but it's really too windy. Maybe tomorrow.'

That was the difference between them. Bill wouldn't have cared. If he needed to buy a shirt and trees weren't blowing over, he would have gone. Yes the wind was strong out there, but not gale force, at least not yet. This was another fascinating subject: the effect that weather had on people, which he supposed had much to do with where you lived, and how much severe weather you experienced. There were those like himself who didn't care. Let it do its worst. It wouldn't last and provided you were sensible, you could carry on regardless. Defiance in a word, like walking outside in torrential rain. Then there were those like Jeanette, who adapted their lives to avoid unpleasant weather, preferring the option of staying indoors when it got nasty. He supposed it depended on how badly you needed to do something. Maybe her visit to the town shopping mall wasn't that urgent anyway, though he knew her well enough to believe that it actually was quite important.

'I'll take you in if you like,' he suggested, knowing she often drove in herself.

'No, really. It can wait. I only want to buy some new saucepans.'

'OK then, but the offer's there if you change your mind.'

The wind grew stronger as the afternoon progressed, and with it the onset of rain. Bill could hear the sound of rain lashing on the back windows. A few hardy, well wrapped, individuals made their way down the road to the corner shop, while the traffic picked up around 3pm for the school run, each car splashing through the growing puddles. The forecasts were severe. A yellow storm warning had been issued for the south west, while southern England, where they lived, could expect heavy weather too in the next twenty four hours. Even Bill felt somewhat relieved at staying indoors this Thursday afternoon, with no appointments till the weekend. He spent the time on some correspondence and later reading a library book on desert landscapes.

Evening saw no sign of the wild weather abating. Bill had already been out to put away the flower pots and secure the bins. The car had earlier been put in the garage. What had been a force seven strong wind this morning was now at least a force nine full gale. Walking was difficult, and he could see a few tiles had fallen from next door's roof. Jeanette took a call from their son, Robert, who reported trees down thirty kilometres away. Daylight was giving way to a murky twilight, and soon it would be dark.

Around 8pm, amid the roar of the storm, Bill switched on the back patio light. His main fear was the greenhouse, some of whose glass panels would doubtless be broken by morning. The legs of the Stevenson's screen were deeply secured in the ground, so it would be fine. He could see stray tree branches at the end of the garden, and a section of fence swaying dangerously. Plans had been made to get this fixed, but the contractor wasn't due for two weeks. There was a good chance it would be down in another hour, and, once exposed, it would put huge pressure on the other sections.

His best chance was to hammer a stake beside the central post to support it. He had some stakes piled at the end of the garden, so getting his waterproofs and toolbox, he braved the storm. First job was to sink the stake deep into the soil beside the concrete base of the post. He hammered it with a mallet, but encountered resistance, maybe a rock. There was no time to dig it out, so he chose another spot, this time with better success. The stake sunk deep into the soil and was near enough to the post that he could secure it with wire in two or three places. Threading the wire round the post took time, as he paused for each gust of wind, some of which nearly blew the post over. Eventually he secured the top tightly, winding the wire around ten times before cutting it and twisting the end. Then he did the middle section, the wire being harder to thread around the back of the post, but four loops were enough. Bill wasn't certain this would hold, but it seemed effective and was all he could do for now.

His battered figure returned indoors and he spent some time surveying his fix. It seemed to hold in what was now a full storm. He let Tracy out briefly but she soon returned in. Turning on the TV, he watched news of trees down, road closures, and rising rivers. It was all too familiar from the storms that had flooded the town two years ago. He felt sorry for those who had to be outside in it – emergency services, home carers, train and bus drivers, though many rail services had already been cancelled. Further phone calls from their two sons assured him that all was well with them. A sudden blast of wind on the front windows shook the whole house. It felt terrifying.

With some nervousness, he retired for the night. He knew Jeanette, always a light sleeper, wasn't going to sleep through this. The howl of the wind continued unabated, even though the rain had stopped. At midnight, Bill got up and put on his heavy coat and boots to check the fence once more. It was holding, not much he could do if it wasn't. The wind was coming now in strong gusts broken by brief pauses. Branches were down next door, but not moving. Relieved, he tried to sleep but woke again at 5am. A large bough had now fallen off the beech tree three doors down, and there looked to be two broken panels on the greenhouse, but no other visible damage. The front drive was all right – a few stray objects, but nothing large or dangerous.

They both rose early, neither able to lie any longer, weary from lack of sleep.

Breakfast was a quiet affair. The worst of the storm had gone, but the wind was still high and swirling, the blasts shorter but still able to hit with a boxer's punch. Neither Jeanette nor he had much to say, it was all in their minds. They could see each other thinking. It was she who broke the silence.

'So how about your walk?'

Bill hadn't thought about it, but even he had to concede that it would be madness to go out in this.

'We'll wait till it's died down. Maybe after lunch.' A deferral - cancellation was out of the question.

It seemed like an admission of defeat, inflicted by mother nature, reminding him in a loud voice not to take herself for granted. Yesterday's wind had been exhilarating, but today's was impossible. Walking in a straight line was just too difficult. Reluctantly he had to admit that. All he could do for now was to wait.

'It'll clear by this afternoon,' he said reassuringly.

'Believe it when I see it.' Jeanette was unconvinced.

'Have you heard the forecast for tomorrow?' he asked out of curiosity.

'Yes, sunny spells.'

Hidden Depths

'How do you start?'

'How do you start anything? Just write what comes into your mind. It's like a big screen that is rubbed clean every few minutes. An idea pops up and colours that space. It needs to be captured before it disappears. Let it flow like a river, from a small spring on a hillside to a raging torrent. Nothing stops it gathering strength and size. Once you grab it, and let it grow, it'll develop into something bigger. All you need to do is keep documenting it.'

'You make it sound so easy. I'm not sure I'm confident enough.'

'It's like swimming. You won't get anywhere standing at the side, admiring the water. There's no choice, you have to jump in. Once you start, it will get easier. And then you can bring in new ideas, link your themes, develop a structure. Look at 'Storm Seekers'.

When I wrote that, I hadn't the faintest notion of how it would end. I didn't even have a title in mind. It started with two boys throwing pebbles in the sea at Blackpool, and went from there. In a strange way, it was like giving birth… it became its own thing, developed its own personality. The baby wasn't going to do what I wanted or expected after a while.'

Trish Chambers, author of six novels and article writer for several magazines, continued to expound to her young listener, Stephanie. There was much to say. Prospective young writers should be encouraged, while tactfully reminded not to be over ambitious. A short story was a good way to start, having a shorter, quicker and more realistic goal. You needed a style, a way to put something across, that differed from everyone else. That was art, the individuality of expression communicating itself to others in the most effective way.

She gave the example of a queue of commuters going home on a Friday evening. One writer could hone in on their blank expressions, caught in the transition between workplace and home, between controlled time and free time. Another could major on the soulless life of the office worker, deprived of the outdoor life, selling his or her soul for a salary. People conditioned by circumstance, leading a life well below their full potential, and craving a window of freedom in the form of a holiday. Something, superficially dull, like a line of commuters waiting for the bus home, becomes transformed into something else that catches our interest, through the power and style of the writer.

While Trish chose to inspire, to enthuse, as a way to break through to her hopeful listener, the effect she had was somewhat different. Stephanie was overawed. Here was an experienced writer waxing lyrical about her past, and how she had worked through difficulty to become successful. High street bookshops stocked Trish Chambers novels, royalties were flowing, and her publisher wanted more. She was already planning the second book of her current trilogy. This meeting in a busy cafe, kindly arranged through the school Old Girls Association, allowed her to unwind and hold forth, making her feel she was showering pearls of wisdom on the next generation, but it wasn't quite succeeding that way.

Stephanie had undeniable potential – English prize at school, stories published in school and university magazines, winner of regional Young Writer competitions, and praised by all. She had made her mark, and received deserved recognition, a flower in the process of blossoming, with yet more to reveal. Now at the point of leaving university and entering the world of work, there was a risk that she would bury her talent as she embarked on a profession in Law, her degree subject, and consign her art to the periphery. Her friends were trying to prevent that, while recognising that she couldn't make a living from writing yet. Part of the problem was that she was a highly skilled young woman, and if her writing didn't develop, there was every chance she would shine in some other field, thus leaving Stephanie the writer behind. She was truly at the crossroads.

They were sitting in "Bruno's", a large restaurant in a Shopping Mall. The place was full of movement: people finding tables, others leaving them, while all around four busy waiters carried trays full of food to waiting groups, and cleaned vacant tables ready for the next customer. Outside, it was a sunny April morning close to Easter, spring was in the air.

Their meeting was like two figures in a painting reaching out to each other, the fingers of each hand stretched forward to meet, but somehow unable to join. What was critical here was a way forward, advice that spelt out the next two or three steps, revealing an onward path. Trish was undoubtedly helpful, her advice sound, but also too strong, and there was still a gap. Her thrown rope didn't quite reach a cautious Stephanie.

'Latte and a cappucino?'

The waiter brought out the two coffees, placing each correctly and then departing with a brief smile.

'Sugar?'

'No thanks,' said Stephanie, as Trish offered the bowl.

Trish would from habit have lit a cigarette, but this was not the place. She paused for a moment in describing how she had changed the plot of 'Street Destiny', while she tore open the sachet and stirred sugar into her latte. While interesting, her monologue was beginning to lose her listener. She too began to sense this, decided to break off and ask a few questions.

'What have you enjoyed writing about so far?'

'I think nature – hills, forests and especially the sea.'

'Why's that?'

'It's so vast. We love the seaside because of the land. It's the only part of the sea we're comfortable with. We can't relate to the vastness and fury of the ocean. It terrifies us.' Stephanie spoke slowly and carefully.

'See there, you have a theme. Fear of the openness of the sea, of being marooned on a raft with endless ocean in all directions. On your own, with no one to help. That's something you can develop into a story. It could even be a dream, developing in a bad way as the swell grows and the raft gets tossed around, and then this huge wave crashes over you. At that point you wake up… but you keep the tension in the story till the last possible moment. Hold that thought. You could make it a short story. There are a number of magazines that would take it, but my advice is to try local ones first, even local papers. At national level, it's very competitive. Everyone fancies themselves as a writer. Build slowly, don't aim for the stars because you'll never get there in one go.'

At last Stephanie was warming to this. All it had needed was an example.

'The sea has many themes – fear, anger, vastness, dominance, monotonousness, drowning, man's impotence to control it. Any of them singly or together can be developed in a story. Think of the Titanic sinking slowly in the Atlantic Ocean, without enough lifeboats, the terror of the passengers left behind. Empty sloping decks awash with fear, where only a few days previously had been laughter and joy. It's a rich treasure chest of ideas. Yes, some have already been used, but there are so many left over.'

'I see,' said Stephanie. 'I can develop some characters, each reacting differently.'

'You want to get known. Enter all the competitions and readings you can. It's hard work but will pay dividends later on. Keep true to your theme. If it's fear of the sea, then that has to be touched on throughout. It's your support, the backbone of your story. Don't try to be spectacular, keep your story believable. You don't need wow factor. It can help, but has to be used wisely.'

Stephanie was making notes. She sipped her cappuccino. The connection had at last been made. This was her next story. Young Writers wanted a three thousand word story for their website, so, if accepted, this could get considerable publicity. Trish spoke of the dangers of repetition in writing, and of always leaving the reader with space to imagine.

The conversation drifted in other directions, back to Trish's challenges and accomplishments, but it had finally achieved its goal. The thirty minutes had gone quickly. Trish stood up to go, offering her card to the grateful Stephanie, and giving her some parting advice:

'And remember, keep a note book. Visit the places you want to write about. Note down feelings, descriptions, ideas. You can expand on these when you write about your subject.'

They went their separate ways, Stephanie making her way back to the family home, a bus ride away. Her head was buzzing. In some ways she was in overload, but the germ of an idea was there. The sea was the way forward. Now she had her motivation, she would make the time to go down to the coast in the next few days.

The following Monday probably wasn't the best time to visit the seaside at Brighton. It was a blustery April morning, with leaden skies and a swell on the waves at high tide. The swirling wind blew empty styrofoam cups and plastic bags down the front, while few people ventured out on to the beach. Apart from an intrepid windsurfer and two tankers on the horizon, there was nothing happening at sea either. Its grey blue mass seethed, while it rhythmically disgorged a succession of waves against the shingle beach, each crashing on impact before being swallowed back into the place it came from.

For Stephanie, it was a matter of hedging her bets, since Brighton had much more to offer than just the beach. A walk along the pier was entertainment itself, while the Aquarium, and old lanes were worth the visit. But her main purpose was to view the sea, note some observations, and find some inspiration for her story.

Trish had stressed the importance of taking care when moving outside the boundaries of experience, less of a problem for her at her age, than for Stephanie, who found the advice a bit confusing. We may not all have visited the seafront when a gale is blowing, but we've watched it on TV enough times to imagine clearly what it's like. Still, a tale of a fishing trip out to sea, or a lost yacht crossing the English Channel into French waters wasn't what Stephanie proposed to cover.

This didn't seem quite the day for inspiration. Cold and windy conditions made it unpleasant, but then again, in some respects, this was ideal. An empty beach made for clear viewing and the rough, swelling sea evoked a feeling of controlled anger, as if an enemy was carefully making their move, reinforcing their troops before a full attack on the town in the form of a gale, with high seas reaching the sea wall. The ultimate would be a tsunami with waves racing through the streets like unleashed dogs, destroying everything in their path. However, that wasn't likely to happen here. The other feeling was about the constancy of nature, as shown by the tides, and the unchanging rhythm of waves. Seas may be changeable, but were locked into the unchangeable.

'Sea'

'Dominant personality.'

This was the first note she made. Nature would have her way whatever happened. It had been proven time and again. Smashed beach huts, eroded cliffs, debris pulled out to sea. It could behave like a capricious monster, at one time personified into Neptune, God of the sea. Docile on a calm sunny day at low tide, but playing a waiting game, ready to pounce and unmask its rage when the opportunity arose. Land by contrast was static, unmoving, like a sleeping elephant, but the sea was always awake and alert, demanding respect at all times. You mistook that at your peril.

Stephanie took a walk along the long pier and looked down at the waves. A piece of timber bobbed along the trough between the slowly forming waves, as if undecided which way it would go. She wondered how much else the sea held, like a big dumping area that avoided the horror of exposure. If we had no sea and could walk three miles out from the beach, what wreckage would we see? Centuries of broken boats, junk thrown overboard, decaying metal, even human skeletons. All washed into some form of respectability over the years, but still identifiable. It prompted her second note:

'Hidden horrors.'

And with that came the thought of the infinity of the sea, miles deep in places, and covering 70% of the world's surface. Below a hundred metres it was dark, monotonous with no landmarks. Like space it went on forever. Was this the ultimate fear, the fear of being lost in this almost bottomless pit? Man's need to relate, to feel secure with a family around him, in one sense helped him survive the awful knowledge that he was, in fact, just a tiny pin among billions that made up human society. Think of that and you go mad. Put some cushion between you and that fact, and you can survive. But being lost in the infinity of the ocean, even if we didn't drown and retained consciousness, was a fear we aren't able to face. Imagine every direction you take, every corner you turn; everything you see is exactly the same.

Nothing varies. There are no clues as to where you are or where you are going. Movement itself has no meaning, and failure to move leads to despair. And so her third note:

'Dark infinity.'

Brief though her notes were, this was probably more than enough for a short story. Each had touchpoints with her visit today, and she spent the rest of the afternoon on pier amusements, eating fish and chips and sampling some fairground rides on the pier. Observations for writing were like brewing beer. The raw materials of a story need to ferment and mature in the mind before a single key could be tapped. Whichever of these three she chose, and it might be more than one, there were ideas and themes to develop, thoughts to verbalise and document, and some thoughts were just impossible to communicate. Words were not enough. All you could do was to present the concept and hope it kicked off in the reader's mind, the same kind of process that it had produced in yours.

A few days passed. Stephanie had some friends to meet, and a leavers' party back at her university city of Nottingham. It gave her the thinking space she needed. She narrowed her focus and began her plot. Her character emerged, and her ending took shape. The next step was time in her room with a newly purchased laptop, to flesh out the detail.

And so it was that Sergei Rushkov, a Russian sailor fell overboard from the "Bayan" while on a naval exercise in the north of the Pacific Ocean. His body was never recovered, assumed drowned. He fell down into the dark ocean depths, where the claustrophobia of low visibility and lack of light, terrified him. He was unable to drown, and so unable to escape. It was like no experience anyone had ever had before. Retaining consciousness was his nightmare, the nightmare of being lost, like looking for a friend on ten million possible crossroads. One will be right, but you haven't a hope of finding which. But Sergei was not just lost, he did not know what to look for if he could escape. His ship was gone, he knew that. He was on his own, no home, no other people to see, in a cold, dark, bottomless place.

Yet gradually, Mother Sea began to care for him, to change his being from one who lived on land, breathed air, ate food and drank water, to one who could survive in the sea and who had no fear, once all knowledge of an earthly life had disappeared. There was no recollection, so there was nothing to fear or desire. There was nowhere to go, so moving aimlessly in the dark, at depths where little marine life existed, didn't matter. Terror came from an earthly perspective, but he was now a creature of the depths.

The sea would sustain him by tuning the wavelength of his mind to accept his lot. Included in this were his bodily needs. He was being reprogrammed to survive on thinking. Fresh thoughts were like food, the mind already used them but now the body could accept them too. The mind fed the body. He began to physically look different, changing from earth man to sea man. He had no needs, no one he had to see. His mental adjustment would affect his longevity too, he would now live at least five hundred years. Sergei would not know land, people, air even if he reached the ocean surface. Floating slowly in the depths was sufficient, no terror, no worries, no desires. For all he knew he was the only one. Nothingness was acceptable and accepted.

It was like something out of science fiction– too fantastic to believe perhaps, but turning perceptions upside down. It looked at the inner being and worked on the most terrifying thing there: fear. The physical situation could not be changed, so the only option left was to change the way we thought about it. Fear comes about because we know something more comforting, more secure. But if we have no knowledge of that, we have nothing to fear. Therefore, we can live with it.

It took Stephanie two full days to write the story, as it flowed out of her in spurts, each followed by a re-read but rarely a correction. First thoughts were good thoughts. She didn't intend a wow factor, it was beyond that, probing the base emotions and needs that mankind relies on. She titled it at first 'Creatures of the Deep', but felt that didn't say it right. So it became 'Sea Man of the Deep.'

She sent it out to a friend for proof reading but soon had it back hardly touched. So it had the thumbs up. Now for Young Writers. She submitted it, expecting a bad review, but they also were cautiously optimistic, scheduling it for publication in two months.

She drew breath. She had never written like this before. The conversion to sea man was almost converting her too. It was a daring piece of writing that took away the boundaries, addressed our fears, and probably broke a few conventions. She smiled inwardly, wondering what Trish would make of it. While Stephanie respected the tips she had been given, it had only confirmed her suspicions that writing was a free for all. There were so many styles and approaches, that no one of these could be declared successful at the expense of others. Writing was about timing, and finding an audience that appreciated your efforts at that time. Like baking bread, it needed freshness and could easily go stale. Successful writers grasped the moment. Yes, they needed skill, but could be helped too if their subject became topical.

She waited in hope, but with an air of confidence. She was discovering herself.

Memories

The flames crackled and flickered like their minds, glowing intensely one minute before dying away again. The warmth and comfort of the large stone hearth drew them together, as if peering into the glow let them see the patterns of their thinking, long periods of inactivity being punctuated by bursts of realisation.

It was a rare meeting for the three of them. As so often happens with siblings, their lives drifted away in separate directions, brought back by the necessities of hospital visiting for sick parents, a family home to clear and sell, or funeral to attend. Even then, family business took priority – banks or solicitors to phone, nursing arrangements to make, house repairs and maintenance to organise. Once a meeting was finished or an arrangement confirmed, they went away again. Usually, it was much easier by phone, rather than in person, so there was no need to meet.

That just left Christmas for catching up, relaxing with a glass of wine and a mince pie in the few hours between lunch and dark, before someone said 'we'd better be getting back' and it was all over till the next time. And so the years rolled on for Philip, or Phil as he preferred to be known, with his teenage daughters now out of university and into careers. Also for Clare with second husband, and a son finishing school, and Emma, the youngest, still single, the one who had lived at home and nursed her father through his years of illness. They were now well into their fifties, ages roughly two years apart.

So here they were on a crisp November day with time, the eternal enemy, for once on their side. A pre-arranged meeting at 'The Barley Mow', Hanningden, a week after their father's funeral, to pause and remember, to get away from undertakers, solicitors, wider family and friends, and just enjoy a quiet drink and lunch. It had been Clare's idea, keenly accepted by the others. She had picked up Emma by car, arriving first, glad to get out of the seasonal cold, and sit by the hearth. Philip entered ten minutes later, removing his scarf and hanging his coat by the door. He ordered a pint of draft beer.

'Ok for drinks?' he asked the others.

'Yes thanks, I'm on my usual' said Emma, eyeing her bacardi and coke.

Clare was on orange juice, aware of having to drive later.

'I had a nice letter from Australia this morning. Uncle George said some nice things about Dad. Here I'll show you.' Clare reached into her bag.

'What's he up to these days?' wondered Phil, 'still at that address in Carine? I don't think he ever left Perth.'

'Yeah… same place.'

'Remember that go-cart he made when we were kids?' This was always the hot button for Phil whenever conversation turned to Uncle George.

'Took him hours, and you crashed it within ten minutes. We won't forget that in a hurry!' Clare smiled at the memory of Phil veering off the downhill path and turning the kart over.

'Couldn't help it, it wouldn't slow down,' Phil defended himself.

'You could so.'

All of a sudden, they burst into laughter. The brief foray into childhood relaxed them all. Like bubbles starting small and growing in size as they reached the surface. There were more to follow.

'I remember it was a shock when he announced he was emigrating to Perth. When we said goodbye he looked so different, stressed and serious, like he didn't really want to do it,' Phil continued.

'I think it was Jane. She just kept on about it. New life, new place. I guess he did it to keep the peace, but I always get the impression he misses the old country,' Clare reflected. Jane was George's wife. They had celebrated their golden wedding last year.

'How many years younger than Dad was he?' asked Emma.

'I'm no good with dates, but Dad was born in 1924, and I think George was three to four years younger, so I guess around 1927.' Clare was the one who remembered the family detail. She had once attempted a family tree going back to the 1820s, much of it based on word of mouth from aging relatives long since dead.

'So he'd be in his eighties now wow, can't imagine him that old! He'd be a young eighty.'

Philip would always remember him with dark hair, shirtsleeves rolled up, and hammer in hand. A frozen frame from the past becoming the image that lasted through the years.

'Dad's other brother, Tom. All we ever had was that portrait photo of him in his RAF uniform.'

'Yes, killed in action 1942,' said Clare, 'we have the newspaper cutting. He would only have been twenty, a bit older than Dad. I think there's a photo of the three of them as kids.'

'Isn't it funny how you never think that a photo someone takes will be so important years later? But it was much more so then, because there were so few photos taken. When they grew up you had to pose in front of a photographer. When we grew up you had the Brownie with 35 mm film. These days it's a click on your mobile phone, take as many as you like, as you can always delete them later.'

'They look so formal – families carefully positioned, hair perfect, and dress immaculate,' observed Emma.

'Yes, and dead pan facial expressions in the older photos. Seems that people relaxed more as photography developed. Oh dear, a pun there! I bet if you told them not to smile, they got the giggles. Probably needed a few retakes knowing Dad,' said Philip, as they all laughed.

'Remember those portrait photos you had at school – tie straight, hair combed. Photographer saying "now look straight at me…say cheese".'

'And one year David Grey stuck his tongue out, and had to go and see Davies.'

'I think it gave him a shock. After all, it was only a joke. The school was making a big thing about disrespect at the time. I think they just wanted a scapegoat. Davies gave him a good talking to apparently. "Boy, what have you done now?"' impersonated Philip.

They broke out laughing again.

'You do him so well, Phil!' exclaimed Clare. 'I haven't thought about any of that for years.'

'Happy Days eh? But certainly not the happiest of your life.'

'No, definitely not. I've enjoyed better.'

A waitress came round to explain the blackboard specials and collect their lunch orders, while pointing them in the direction of the Dining Room. They ignored the hint, being reluctant to leave the fireside. Somehow it was galvanising the conversation.

'Tell you what I came across the other day,' said Clare, 'since we're talking about photos….. some old black and white snaps from that holiday in Broadstairs. They were in the back of a drawer in the study.'

'What year would that have been?'

'Gosh, let me think… maybe 62 or 63. It was before we had a car.'

'There's one of us at the beach on donkeys. I remember Phil falling off his. This photo must have been taken minutes before that happened. I remember Mum being really worried, and taking him into Margate to have his arm checked. We were thinking 'Is that it? Will we have to go home?"

Phil's recollection was a lot vaguer. He was the accident prone member of the family, and had been left with several scrapes and near misses from childhood. This had not been the worst incident.

'Don't remember much about it, probably just the shock,' he volunteered.

'Oh come on Phil, how can you forget that!' Emma was dumbfounded.

'All I remember is that it rained most days and the ice cream seller in Viking Bay. I worked hard on persuading Dad to buy us an ice cream each day, but I think I only won once. He kept telling me that I'd get it when I showed I could finish the dinner they served at that place we stayed. And I never did. Just didn't like the food much, and the portions were so large. I think on the last day he took pity on me and let me win.'

'You're the eldest Phil. You should remember more than us,' said Emma. 'Even though I was only four, there's probably two things that stick in my mind – the beige trellised pattern wallpaper in the bedroom, like an optical illusion, and the big blue bucket we used for making sandcastles. I think that's where we bought it, as I know we had it for years afterwards. Oh yes and Matilda Bear.'

'Matilda?' groaned Clare, 'you two were inseparable till you were at least ten. Remember when she got lost and you nearly screamed the place down. I think Dad found her days later under a bush in the garden.'

'Forget what happened to her,' said Emma. 'I know I couldn't bear to give her away, emotional value and all that. Oh sorry, another terrible pun!'

'There was something about a walk that I recall.' Clare spoke deliberately as she stared into the fire. 'I think Mum wanted us to walk up to the lighthouse and have a look round. Must have been one of the afternoons when it stopped raining. I had no idea what lighthouses were used for. It just seemed a good place to climb up to the top and get a good view.'

'Wow I had forgotten all about that,' said Phil. 'Now you mention it, I do recollect climbing those narrow steps. I didn't have a head for heights, so it was a bit scary.'

'I don't even remember it. Was I with you?' asked Emma.

'Yes, I think so. Maybe Mum stayed with you, while we went up. Probably thought you were too small. She was always safety conscious.'

'Didn't we play cricket with the other family from the Guest House, against those two boys who were older than us. We kept losing the ball 'cos they whacked it into the garden next door.' Phil's memory was beginning to thaw. 'One of them bowled really fast. I don't think any of us got runs off him, just painful LBWs.'

'Don't remember,' said Clare. 'It's funny how you can recall things that I'd forgotten, and vice versa. It needs the three of us to put the complete puzzle together. Actually no… we only have a fraction of it. We'd need Mum or Dad back to complete it. So most of what happened that holiday is permanently forgotten now. Not that it matters.'

'Just strange how you remember some tiny detail,' added Philip, 'like Dad opening the railway carriage door and lifting two suitcases inside. I do remember that. It was because I was thinking: what happens if the train leaves before we all get on? I was scared about being last and getting left behind on the platform. The things you think about as a kid!'

'And the smell of those carriages, like a mix of stale cigarette smoke, grease and dust. You just got used to it, like the blue smoke on the upstairs deck of a double decker bus in the 60s and 70s. These days, it would be unheard of! We're probably all victims of passive smoking, but you never thought anything of it then.'

The waitress called them over while placing hot steamy dishes of vegetable curry and beef lasagne on their table. Despite the central heating, it felt cold away from the warmth of the hearth. They ordered a half bottle of Chablis while eating slowly, the conversation still in flow.

'Dad used to give us sixpence pocket money when I was really young,' said Emma, 'then it went up to a shilling, and eventually two and a half shillings. Half a crown I think it was called. Never saw a full one. A pound was a big thing, twenty shillings. That could be twenty weeks saving. These days it's nothing.'

'You had that pink piggy bank. You were forever counting your money, like you were training to be a bank teller,' remarked Clare.

'I think it was counting those shillings, and knowing what I wanted once I got my first pound saved. There was this doll I wanted with different costumes you could get. Every shilling counted, and birthday money too. Working out how long to wait before you could go to the toy shop.'

'Same with the train set,' observed Phil. 'The track was quite cheap but the rolling stock was anything from three shillings upwards. A turntable was ten shillings, a small fortune. You had to work out what you wanted most and go for that first. See I can remember clearly those prices from years ago, but ask me how much a bottle of Coke costs today, and I couldn't tell you.'

'I guess it taught us to value money. A purpose to waiting. There was a real thrill when you walked into the shop, counted out your money and watched them wrap up your purchase. Then opening it up at home, undoing the box, holding whatever it was, and playing with it.'

'Toys were it!' exclaimed Phil emphatically. 'I can remember getting puffin paperback books for Christmas and being so disappointed. And then you had to write a nice letter to Auntie whoever to say thank you for something you didn't really want. Felt like giving her a bit of advice for next year, but Mum started to get annoyed, and said I should learn to be grateful. If it was a model plane kit, I would have been.'

'That's so you Phil,' said Emma smiling, 'at least your honest enough to admit it!'

'And then there were the gifts you got that looked promising from the outside but turned out to be a box of handkerchieves. So disappointing. They were the last thing you wanted, let alone having to be grateful for it. There should be a rule that says socks and handkerchieves can't be gift wrapped on account of the acute disappointment suffered by most recipients upon opening the gift.'

The girls burst into hysterics.

'There are women who would love a wrapped lace handkerchief.' Emma responded.

'I said "most" recipients, not "all". I don't know any teenage boy who would be an exception.'

'What'll you think of next – issuing gift lists for Christmas presents like people do for their weddings? I bet they're pleased to get handmade linen handkerchieves!'

'Clare, I've made the point.'

They were back to their old selves, trying on childhood roles like old gloves. Phil the spoilt brat, Clare the mediator, and Emma, the baby, looking up to her elder brother and sister, while trying to follow their conversations.

The two portions of vegetable curry and rice, and the lasagne were duly finished. Desserts and coffee were ordered.

'Can't remember the last time the three of us sat down for lunch – must have been some chance occasion when we were all home, between university terms. We certainly haven't been out for lunch for ages. I guess having Dad nursed at home for years prevented that,' reflected Clare. 'Just feels so good to be here chatting. That's families. You all go your separate ways, but have this common bond. You spend all your time with partners, children, friends, business acquaintances, but keep returning to your siblings. You can choose a husband, but not a brother, but having choice doesn't make it better somehow. Family teaches you so much.'

'I agree totally,' said Emma. 'Something about the formative years too. That's when you learn so much, and when the people you're close to matter so much. You're all in it together, and that itself makes a bond that lasts, let alone the blood ties you have.'

'Yes, when it works, there's nothing stronger. You can leave it be for years and it's still there to come back to, like invisible glue.'

They drained their coffee cups, and paid the bill. It was time again to go their separate ways, but somehow each seemed reluctant to go. The fireside drew them back invitingly, as if it was there for them alone. They were indeed almost the only occupants in the lounge.

Sitting in silence for a few minutes, they each thought about their father, with none quite able to verbalise anything. This wasn't about sadness. He had enjoyed a full life until the indignity of dementia had left him to endure a captive existence for the last two years of his life, both physically and mentally. He would have loved being here today in a pub he used to frequent with friends and family, and would have approved of his three children enjoying the ambience of the log fire, and the pleasure of shared memories.

Phil was the first to rise.

'Better head home I guess, though I could stay here all afternoon. It's been a pleasure.'

He embraced them both, put on his coat and waved goodbye.

A few minutes later, Clare and Emma got up, and made their way to the car, glancing back at the crackling fire, as if to stamp it on their memories.

The engine revved.

And so it was over. Special moments in the life of a family. Only a few hours, so precious, yet so rare.

Choice

She could see the junction at the brow of the hill ahead, and walked more slowly as she approached it, as if aware of its importance. This required full concentration, for the way forward was unclear and there were different routes to take. No road sign would help Sonia now, despite the direction always being forward, because she did not know her destination, or indeed the next place on the way. It had been easier up till now. There had been the camaraderie of friends to enjoy as together they all took the right fork rather than the left, or took the left turn at the crossroads rather than the right, but now they had gone their separate ways, and she had walked some distance on her own. Even though she had talked about the journey and route intersections with older friends and family, when it came to being at a junction it was you and you alone. There was no such thing as second hand experience.

Or was she alone?

As Sonia approached the crossroads, it became clear there were three ways forward, a wide road ahead forking to the right down the other side of the hill, a steeper narrower road to the left twisting up the hill, and a small laneway into the forest on the right. Each was different, and there would be no prospect of return. The choice, right or wrong, would be made first time. The landscape had a pristine, natural appearance, the rocky outcrops of the mountain ridge contrasting with the thick pine forest that enveloped the foreground. Beyond the ridge, the forest fell away to grassy plains. Man for once had made no impact.

Ahead, she also saw an old man sitting on a bench. He smiled at her, as if to allay any fears that she might have, and waited for her greeting.

'Hello, who are you?' she asked.

'My name is Pengist. I was once a eye surgeon, and performed many operations to make people see,' he responded.

'So what are you doing here?'

'I am old now, but come back to help others to see their lives with clearer vision. They talk to me, sometimes for days, before they move on. Perhaps, I can help you too.'

He was dressed like a monk, making him a rather surreal figure, his thick white bushy hair and beard giving him an air of authority. A weathered face spoke of experience, and thin quick fingers of capability. He continued.

'I, too, came here but it was many years ago, and like you now, I had to decide. There is no right and wrong way, but whichever route you choose will direct your life. You have to think of everything, big or small before deciding. No computer program will help you. There is no magic formula, no safety net. You have to take the risk.'

'But I don't know which way to go! I would probably just carry on down the other side of the hill,' Sonia exclaimed.

'Which is why we have to talk. You have other opportunities now, and you should notice them. There is no hurry, but once you choose you cannot return, because you will never be the same person again. Come sit down.'

He beckoned to the bench where he was sitting, and after hesitating, she took up his invitation.

'Tell me about yourself. I don't even know your name.'

'Sonia… Sonia Matthews, I'm twenty two, a year out of college, working part time at a local newspaper because there was nothing else. I've been living at home, but want to move out. I just need to get a bit more money together.'

'I see… I see,' repeated Pengist as he absorbed the information. He gave the impression of having six questions to ask, but settled on one. 'Tell me, where are you going?'

'I don't really know. I was just continuing the journey after leaving my friends. Maybe I was half expecting new friends to join, but no one's shown up yet. I've been on my own the last couple of days.'

'Do you mind that?'

'Well it made a change at first, but now, well I was beginning to wonder where everyone is?'

Pengist smiled to himself.

'They all come through here at some point,' he said. 'Some of them charge straight on down the hill, hardly saying a word. I live in a small hut on the mountainside, and come down here to talk to travellers. People are so different. No two days are the same for me.'

'So how can you help me?' Sonia asked the million dollar question.

'By helping you to help yourself. You're young, and have your life in front of you. You'll leave home, make new friends, travel the world, meet Mr Right, marry, have your own family – a so called successful life. But then again, maybe you won't. Who defines success anyway?'

'But I haven't thought about any of that. It's years ahead,' Sonia protested.

'Things can happen quickly in life, you'd be surprised. But anyway, let me ask you another question: what do you believe in? Think carefully before replying.'

Sonia paused. It reminded her of an Ethics lecture at university, having her values challenged.

'Freedom, family, love if you find the right person.'

'OK that's a start.' Pengist was warming to the conversation. 'Now which of those do you feel most passionate about?'

'None really. I suppose freedom. Love can hurt as I found out with my last boyfriend. You trust people who let you down. But I'd hate to live in a world that controlled my life – told me what to eat, where to go, what to think. I think being free to choose, matters.'

'Ok hold the thought.' He seemed positively excited. 'What can you do to protect freedom?'

'Use my vote, demonstrate, campaign to protest about suppressed news reporting, e-spying, phone tapping and so on. Well that's a start.'

'Yes, until politicians let you down, and you realise that governments have been spying on you for years. The real issue is trust. No one likes being deceived.' Pengist was getting more direct.

Sonia stood up and walked around. This was getting less comfortable. She hadn't expected to have her values challenged, and couldn't see what all this had to do with choosing the right road to take. Was Pengist just playing devil's advocate? Maybe she shouldn't have stopped. He was playing games with her.

'I'm just trying to show you that freedom can be an illusion,' he went on. 'We think we're free to do what we want, but in reality we have little control. You have to be wary, and careful with others. Trust is a beautiful thing. Hand it out like gold. You will trust a lot less in life than you will love. You can love many, and love is also a precious gift, but trust few. Let people win your trust.'

He had hit the spot. Sonia was inclined to trust everyone, until they let her down, but she had recently been re- evaluating that in the light of experience. Trust had to be earnt, and given sparingly.

'How do you know who to trust?' she asked him.

'Your head can never tell you, it comes from the heart. Like love, you know in your heart if it's right. The most precious things in life are from the heart – love, faith and trust. They sit close to one another. Your head can never tell you to have faith, to look beyond the boundary of hope, and believe so strongly in something or someone that you don't think to doubt.'

'You make it sound wonderful,' Sonia was listening to every word.

'Belief comes from the head. You can prove or disprove the logic in a statement, even conduct an experiment. If it works, believe it. Others will too. It's scientific proof. Faith, however, comes from the heart. You just know inside you that something is right, or that someone will come good. Only you can work that out, because there is no proof. Others will also have their faith, but not your faith. It's personal to you. I'm talking about faith with a small 'f' as well as religious faith with a capital 'F'. Faith is not an emotion. The emotions are a roller coaster, constantly changing – joy, anger, fear going up and down, and taking you for the ride. Faith is much more constant. It's real, you don't have to feel in the mood for it. You sense it and know it rather than feel it. It's always there, coming from your heart.'

She sat down again, absorbing everything he was saying. It seemed to ring true, and that itself was a message from the heart. He made it sound as if the heart was so much more important than the head. The latter she could relate to from the university lecture halls, but faith was something she had never really known. She had never been religious, but remembered vividly visiting a Catholic church as a child, and seeing the suffering Christ on a big wooden cross over the altar. The image had been one of pain, whilst in a place of complete peace. As if that pain was somehow only understandable in the midst of peace, and needed to be understood. Faith and love stood side by side that day, inseparable.

'And what of love?' she asked him.

'Loving someone, that special person in your life, is an act of the heart, and also an act of faith. You have faith in them. Having faith in God is a more perfect example. Human love will fade and get hurt. You will lose the faith you once had in a lover, though eventually you may meet someone who offers dependable love. God however won't let you down. You may change the relationship you have with Him as your experiences in life change, but He is constant and offers love, hoping for a response. If accepted, the relationship can last for years, even eternity. Faith is not love. We make decisions in faith that don't need love, like choosing a career path or a place to live, just as we can love our family without needing to exercise faith, but the two often go together.'

'I have faith in certain things, like the power of nature,' admitted Sonia.

'We exercise faith more than we think – it's not a word we use much. It's different from belief because we believe what is logical. We go to buy bread in the supermarket because we believe, from past experience, that we can get bread there. We don't go as an act of faith. Faith goes beyond that. It needs vision and takes risk. Building a hospital is an act of faith, faith that the power of healing ultimately beats all the forces that can prevent the hospital being built – lack of resources, delays, corruption, opposition, lack of available medical staff. If we took no risk, there would be no hospital. You can say that we're using public money, so the risk is spread, but what about the first hospitals, and the vision it took to start them? Someone knew in their heart that it was the right thing to do, and took the risk.'

'Yes, I see what you mean.'

There was much to digest here, and much of what Pengist said made sense, but she hadn't thought about it in that way before. This was intense. Part of her wanted a break, to move around, let her head settle, but she also didn't want to break her concentration, and he didn't look like the kind of person to take time out.

'So where does religious faith come into this?' she asked him.

'That is the ultimate faith you exercise. It underlies everything. You can have faith in the ultimate triumph of good over evil in different forms or religions. God is constant, we are inconstant. We blame God when things go wrong, but forget that there is no assumption in life that they always go right. We are both sitting here talking now, but could both be dead tomorrow. Life is transient. Religious faith becomes a form of security, but is more than wanting to believe in God. Look at Christianity. In it faith is a way of life – you offer in faith, live by faith, observe the power of faith, and receive in faith. Instead of being a marginal activity that we think of now and again, it becomes the centre of your life. You can only know that from exercising it. No one can do it for you.'

Sonia was back at the Catholic church in her mind. The beautifully carved and painted stations of the cross had left her in awe of something, but she wasn't sure what. The deep serenity, sitting in silence and feeling at peace had been brief, like a deep dive, but left a lasting impression. It was placed somewhere in the mind's labyrinth, ready to be called on, like right now. For a moment there was nothing she could say.

Pengist, sensing her struggle, waited. Words had stopped for now. He beckoned her to follow him up a narrow twisted path towards his hut. The short walk stopped at a lookout point just off the path. This gave a much better view of the junction, by looking down over it. They gazed at the fork in the road, and the turning off to the right for some minutes. Eventually he broke the silence, speaking quietly.

'Each of the three ways ahead are paths of life. You are at a place where you have to exercise faith in making your choice. Everyone has to, there is no alternative, but they may not recognise that. That's because what you choose now will determine the rest of your life. You are twenty two years old, and have important decisions to make about career and moving out of home. You could apply for a job in business, perhaps as a Marketing Consultant, have a good salary, rent a flat for a few years before you buy your own home. Or you could work as a charity volunteer in an African country for a few years, sacrificing wealth to help people, or you could travel the world, sample different cultures, and emigrate. There are many options open to you. One is not necessarily better than others, but you are in a position to choose, and whichever choice you make will determine many things in your life. You can cross over from one path to another, but as you can see, it's not easy. The further you go, the harder it gets.'

He paused a moment.

'You can't know right now which is the best path. No one can. We don't have hindsight to help us, and in life we cannot go backwards. But faith and vision can help, and whichever way you choose, they will remain with you, if you let them. The decision of which route you choose is separate from the decision of how you go forward, and having faith can, and does, apply to all three. You've passed through other junctions before, but this one is important. It's a junction of life. There will be others later. You have this opportunity to make changes and switch direction, and you should be aware of that. Think laterally, think positively. It must be an informed choice.'

Sonia nodded in silence. Speech was, for now, beyond her. Had she not met him, she would doubtless have continued on the wide road bearing right over the hill. It rose gradually towards a gap in the hills, and beyond to the plain ahead, keeping a straight direction as the forest gave way to grassland. The steeper road to the left, although requiring more effort, gave better views as it climbed out of the forest. As if the greater effort gave greater reward. It went up the mountain till it met a ridge along which it ran into the distance. The small road off to the right penetrated into the heart of the forest. She could see it winding down to a river in a meandering way, before continuing over the other side as a narrow track. This would be a totally different experience, more lonely, needing more strength. It was somehow more fascinating, more on the edge.

Pengist looked her in the eye and held out his right hand.

'I have no more to say, other than to wish you well. You can take your time in deciding your way forward. I am not here to influence but to inform. Do you have anything more to ask?'

She shook her head, and then smiled weakly, as he turned away from her. He made the slow climb towards his hut, while Sonia walked back to the cross roads. She stopped for a few minutes and sat down again, shutting her eyes to aid concentration.

Had he confused or clarified the choices? Was he right about everything or somehow just able to impress? Was the right turn worth the risk? Was the left fork too much like hard work, or should she just go with the flow and carry on the main road?

The best way to decide was to sleep on it, and besides it was getting dark. She found a patch of ground to pitch her tent, and lay in it sleepless for hours, tossing and turning.

At first light, she woke, packed her tent and walked down her chosen route.

Time Off?

'There's free Wi-Fi, Dad.'

'OK so you should have no problems. Do you know the password?'

'It's in the room folder. First thing I looked for.'

James was talking to Jenny his daughter, who was trying to connect her laptop in the room. The family summer holiday in a small hotel would be incomplete if offline. She had bought a stack of PC games and DVDs but still wanted her favourite websites.

'Can I ask something?' inquired James.

'Yuh' she was busy trying the password. 'OK yes I'm in. What?'

'Do you ever back up your hard drive?'

Jenny looked blank.

'Back up? No.'

'So what would you do if you went to power up your laptop one day and the screen showed some strange code indicating a disk failure?'

'Dunno, get it repaired or get a new laptop I suppose.' She didn't seem too concerned.

'Yes, but you'd have lost all your files. Your programs would be OK, you just re-install them from the CDs or website downloads but everything you've created since your last backup, if there was one, would be gone.' James hoped he was driving the point home, but wasn't sure he was succeeding. He had, in fact, made a recent back up of her machine himself so knew all would not be lost, but wasn't disposed to let her off the hook.

'Yeah… see what you're saying. Probably a good idea.' Jenny was giving him half her concentration so the point was lost.

'So much of your life is in that box. Think of the time you've invested in homework assignments, all the arty stuff you do, you know card design and so on. You've had the PC two years now and used it heavily. It's a durable item, but what if you dropped it? Or spilt drink over it? One accident could ruin the machine.' James was determined to push the point.

'See what you mean Dad. You're right, but can we worry about that when we get home?'

'We'll probably have to as we don't have an external hard drive or memory stick here. But you should be thinking about this yourself. It's not a Daddy job.'

James let it go there. He was somewhat out of favour with bringing a personal computer on holiday anyway, preferring a holiday away from the computer. Homes were like offices these days. You powered the office machine down at 5pm only to power up the home laptop two hours later, admittedly for different purposes, but the environment was the same. Surely a week's holiday by the sea could give them a total break, but maybe that was being too unrealistic. There was always a reason to go online, and he himself might need to, thus breaking his own theory. Perhaps he just enjoyed finding something to be disagreeable about.

It was getting late and he returned next door to the double room. His wife Linda was already unpacking suitcases, filling the chest of drawers in her organised way. He made some tea for them both, while looking at the view of the sea front from the window. Well this was it, the long awaited July break. When it came to holidays, they were unambitious. Others could enjoy Majorca or the Canaries, but Bournemouth at this time of year ticked the box for the three of them. It was three years since they were last here. They looked forward to visiting the same old haunts, eating in their favourite restaurants, and chatting about nothing in particular. Indeed doing nothing had a certain appeal to it. Taking time over meals, walking along the promenade, or even sitting on the beach - all seemed attractive. Switching off, rather than running to a schedule, was the key.

'Forecast looks good for tomorrow. Let's have a nice slow day.' Linda broke from the unpacking to sit in the armchair and drink the tea he had prepared.

'Yes, sounds ideal.'

'Meant to tell you, changing the subject remember that restaurant I went to last week with work?' she continued. 'Well just next to us was a table of six, three couples, who spent all evening messing around with their mobile phones. As if that was more important than talking to each other.'

'I'm not surprised, you do see it increasingly. Really, I can't see the point of meeting people for dinner if you don't give them your time. Phones become addictive. It's like you're physically with a group of people, but are actually mentally with others. Rude really but becoming socially acceptable. We all do it to an extent but need to know when to cut off.' James felt his comment was honest rather than self righteous.

'Can't see the point of meeting. Society has to be so interactive. With email you expect a reply sometime when convenient, but these days everything is about chat. You make a comment and expect one back within minutes, regardless of where and what the other person's doing.'

'Remember Dad?' smiled James. 'He used to say the phone is rude because it demands an immediate answer. You'd be in deep conversation with someone, and have to cut off when the phone rang. Of course you could just let it ring, but then it could be someone important. Then you'd get back to the conversation and say "yes where were we?" but somehow the momentum was lost.'

'Well he's right,' asserted Linda, 'very right. Of course the caller can't know what the other person is doing right then, but it's easier now with caller identification and voice mail. I guess you just respond to the ones you want to, but have to be careful. Good chance you'll ring back and the person's unavailable. And people don't often leave a full message, they just say please call me back. You can't know how important a call is till you connect and listen to it. The one you don't answer will often be the important one.'

'Like a cry for help that you never responded to. And we've all wanted it too. You've been in a road accident, needed to tell someone, needed that friend to calm you down right then,' added James.

'Indeed. When we were young, that would have been a public call box if you weren't in shock and more likely a call hours later when you finally got home.' Linda sipped her tea. 'I suppose it's all about the instant gratification society, but you have to have the strength to cut off from it. Back to the restaurant It's the will to leave it aside for a couple of hours. Maybe this group were the extreme. It's all about striking a balance I suppose.'

The conversation wandered on to other matters. One of the benefits of being away from home and distractions was the opportunity to talk. The daily business of living often carried an economy of conversation, enough to get through the tasks of the day like 'what do you want for dinner?' Away from there, and in a new less demanding setting, you could open up.

Monday a bright sunny day, saw them drive down to Studland beach, relaxing on the sand with a view of the Isle of Wight in the distance. After a brief swim and a walk around the bay, they settled on a shady spot and spread the car rug. Linda laid out the packed lunch she had prepared - salad sandwiches, bananas, yoghurt.

'Nice to see you both relax,' she said encouragingly.

James had just finished the paper, though rather wished he hadn't bought it. News had a habit of being bad – fighting in Syria, Iraq, an earthquake in Indonesia, a disappearing plane, presumed crashed in a remote mountain range. He felt a responsibility to keep in touch with world events, to be shocked with bad news, to donate to famine appeals, but became weary of the continued violence and death that never seemed to disappear, and much of which seemed preventable.

'What would happen to us if we lost interest in the news?' he asked.

'How do you mean Dad?'

'Well it's always so depressing. I'm not trying to be selfish because we should know what's happening and it might affect us. But what would happen if we didn't watch the news, buy newspapers, listen to radio. Tune out in other words.'

'Well it would still happen, but you'd eventually feel cut off and bewildered because you wouldn't know the world around you.' Linda commented. 'We live in a global village. Climate change for example affects us all, and individually we adapt our behaviour, maybe subtly, to what we hear and see in the media. If you had a son in the army and he was put on alert to go to Afghanistan, you'd want to know what was going on there. If you wanted to visit a country that had problems, knowing what was going on there would affect your decision to go and your safety when you arrived there.'

'Yes, I guess you're right. I suppose the bad stories tend to be about events. A plane crashing is news. A plane landing safely isn't. Steady growth in the economy isn't newsworthy or headline grabbing, but is good for everyone. Happy family reunions fall below the radar too.' James was philosophical.

'It's also an interest for us. It's how we relate to the world. You feel you know the celebrities and football stars. A bit of a one-sided relationship as they don't know us, but we can relate through daily updates. Instantly you can see what others are up to. That can inspire as well as depress.'

'True, true. Maybe it's just a bad day to pick up the paper.'

'Turn to the crossword or sodoku instead,' suggested Linda.

'No it'd be a bit sad to come down here and spend two hours solving those. Think I'll enjoy the Dorset scenery while I'm here. Who's for a walk up the headland?'

'Let's all go. Looking at some trees and rocks will sort your head out. Throw that newspaper away.'

Linda packed away the lunch, and they set off on the trail at the back of the beach towards Old Harry Rocks, and the chalk downs. The array of purple, yellow and white wildflowers en route was the perfect tonic for unburdening minds.

'Dad what does a grebe look like?' asked Jenny.

'Haven't a clue. Would need to look it up.' James was no ornithologist.

'Can you check now?'

'Yes guess so.' He googled it on his phone, noticing Linda laughing.

'Here you are darling.' He showed the image to Jenny before turning to his wife.

'What's so funny about that?'

'Instant gratification, taking a rest from technology because you're on holiday!'

'Oh yes… well… snookered there!'

'And it won't be the only time. I'll start counting!' She insisted on rubbing it in.

Old Harry Rocks looked dazzling white in the sunshine, three stacks of chalk teeming with birds. Having taken the obligatory photo, they returned to Studland village for afternoon tea, and then drove back to the hotel.

'You haven't mentioned the "G" word yet,' said Linda.

'"G" word? What do you mean?'

'Gets an airing every holiday. Do I have to give you a clue?'

It took a few moments to sink in.

'Oh you mean golf! Well I didn't bring any clubs this time. But we can still do a pitch and putt,' replied James, determined not to be outdone.

'Well maybe you and Jenny. I can't say my form has improved much.' Linda wasn't to be drawn.

'Maybe later in the week. To be honest I'm not fussed. Plenty else to do down here.'

'Anything you say dear,' Linda yawned.

Sure enough Wednesday morning saw James teeing off on the first hole at a local course. Golf wasn't his forte as he would be the first to admit, but he liked to keep his hand in, and the beauty of playing with the family now was that no one was going to get upset with their form. Besides, a nine hole pitch and putt course wasn't exactly the links at the local club. They each hired a 7 iron and putter.

His tee shot with the iron on the first hole was a healthy smack which sent the ball in a huge arc towards the green, landing just on the edge. As if over-confident with his start, he proceeded to tell Jenny how to hold the club.

'Da-ad! I have done this before you know.'

'A little advice never went astray,' responded James.

Her scuffed shot sailed towards the right and landed a third of the way down the fairway.

Linda, after some last minute persuasion, had decided to make up the three. Her self deprecation masked the fact that she was a reasonable player with a good eye, especially when putting. Despite a weak tee shot, she was on to the green with her second shot.

James hit a par three, Linda a four and they waited a while Jenny painstakingly made her way up the fairway finishing with a seven.

'OK, that's just practice. I'll catch up.'

'I'm worried,' muttered James jokingly.

The next two holes saw the gap narrowed as James missed a two foot putt, while Jenny managed a par at the third.

The fourth required some care, there being a lake to the left, and a large bunker strategically positioned to the right. It was a choice between a gentler iron shot from the tee to land short of the bunker, followed by a chip over and up on to the green, or else try and blast it over the top from the tee. Skill, however, lay not in power.

James, yet to have a serious setback, opted for the latter, probably thinking 'that this can't happen to me'. His swing hit under the ball and sent it skywards rather than forward. It made a perfect arc and landed right in the bunker.

'Thought you would have avoided that, Dad?' Jenny wasn't going to let the opportunity slip.

'OK, you show us how it's done then.' James wasn't to be silenced.

And indeed she did. Her tee shot slightly to the left fell well short of the bunker and with a good line of sight to the green. Linda followed with a similar shot and they both finished with par 4.

James made two unsuccessful attempts to get out of the bunker, then over hit the green and finished with a seven, his face etched with frustration.

'Having problems there darling?' Linda sounded the innocent.

'Don't you start.'

'Let's see the scores, could be getting close.'

James still led, but only by a single shot, with Linda second and Jenny two shots behind her. A close contest for the remaining five holes.

Calamity struck again at the sixth hole when Linda, in a rare lapse, miscued a drive into the woods.

'Who's going to get that?' James asked.

'Don't know. Are you offering?'

'You lose two shots for a lost ball, and start again well into the rough.'

'I'm sure I'm not the first. The place is probably awash with lost balls.'

Sure enough she found one, and whacked it hard out of the rough to catch them up.

After seven holes, James led by two shots, with Jenny now second and Linda three shots behind her. As ever with courses, the eighth hole was the anti-climax before the grand finale, a longer hole with a right hand bend that required care so as not to overshoot the corner.

James and Jenny both dropped a shot on the eighth, while Linda shot par, so it was all to play for on the final hole.

Linda went first, restraining her shot so as to clear the bend with her second. Jenny had the same idea, but mishit and watched the ball trickle a few yards from the tee while James tried to clear the bend in one shot, hitting a tree and seeing his ball ricochet back across the fairway and well into the left hand rough.

'Now who's trying to be clever?' ribbed Linda.

Her second shot was immaculate landing a few yards from the hole, while Jenny made up for her error, making the centre of the green in two more shots. James, his annoyance showing, needed two shots to clear the rough, and three more to get home. Jenny's four and his six were enough to tie the leader scores with Linda two shots behind.

'Good game everyone,' said James encouragingly.

'Thought you were home and dry Dad,' smiled Jenny.

James wouldn't admit to having expected to win, but had high hopes especially after a good start. It was the classic case of a friendly game with a slightly serious edge, and a few regrets at missed chances.

'You played well. Improved as the game went on,' he said charitably.

'Time for lunch,' said Linda. 'Where shall we head to?'

'How about fish and chips on the front?'

'Good idea.'

'I only charged that an hour ago, and the battery's almost flat.'

It was the morning of their last day, and James was checking his mobile phone.

'Order a new battery when we get home, dear. You won't need to use it here. Remember our conversation?' Linda found amusement in his predicament.

'Yes' he said with a wry smile. 'You're right, who do I need to ring anyway? If it's important, they'll call me.'

'Holidays are about cutting off, but actually we're uncomfortable doing that,' she observed. 'If someone said you have to surrender your watch, phone, and car keys at the start of your holiday, what would you say?'

'Well I'll tell you,' she continued, 'you'd say the holiday wouldn't be complete without them. But actually, you don't need to be anywhere at a certain time, you can use public transport or just not go too far, and you can tell your friends you're away and ask them not to call, text or email you for a week.'

'Well I suppose so.'

'But actually you expect to be bothered. If you didn't get ten emails a day, or look at social media, you'd feel uneasy, so you're prepared to accept some interruptions. It's like silence, we're uncomfortable with it, but it's the perfect healing for a fulfilling holiday. Have you ever tried listening to silence, it sounds really loud.'

James had to acknowledge there was truth in what she said, and that while he paid lip service to it, he was as much part of the problem as part of the solution. Holidays should start with removing something, so that there was space to allow something else to take its place. Instead of that, they became an extra layer on top of everything else we do, and while we enjoyed them, we often don't get the most out of them.

It was also about getting out of 'doing' mode into 'being' mode, made easier if you do nothing each day, and forget about time. While less memorable, those are the days that do you the most good.

'All very philosophical… now where were we… oh yes… a day trip to the Isle of Wight. Why not? How do we book and where do we have to be for the ferry? Let's make the last day memorable!' exclaimed James.

About The Author

Andrew Rees was born and brought up in Bromley, Kent but has spent time overseas including sixteen years in Sydney, Australia. He returned to the London in 1999, and raised his two children there, but now lives in Cheltenham UK. While working in Information Technology for a career, he started writing books twenty years ago. He has published 'Light Places' (2006), 'Running Over' (2009). 'Touchpoints' is his first book of short stories, inspired by experience, observation and the knowledge that we all have a story in us waiting to be told. Together they make a strong chorus.

www.ingramcontent.com/pod-product-compliance
Lightning Source LLC
Chambersburg PA
CBHW021335190726

48288CB00003B/1123